Romeow and Juliet

by

Kathi Daley

This book is a work of fiction. Names, characters, places, and incidents either are products of the author's imagination or are used fictitiously. Any resemblance to actual events or locales or persons, living or dead, is entirely coincidental.

This book is dedicated to the people I met during my trip to the San Juan Islands to research this series, especially Shannon Borg, who took the time to answer my questions and introduce me around.

I also want to thank the very talented Jessica Fischer for the cover art.

Special thanks to Vivian Shane, Connie Correll, Joyce Aiken, Melissa Nicholson, and Robin Coxon for submitting recipes.

And, of course, thanks to the readers and bloggers in my life who make doing what I do possible.

And, as always, love and thanks to my sister Christy for her time, encouragement, and unwavering support. I also want to thank Carrie, Cristin, Brennen, and Danny for the Facebook shares, Randy Ladenheim-Gil for the editing, and, last but not least, my super-husband Ken for allowing me time to write by taking care of everything else.

Books by Kathi Daley.

Zoe Donovan Cozy Mystery:

Halloween Hijinks
The Trouble With Turkeys
Christmas Crazy
Cupid's Curse
Big Bunny Bump-off
Beach Blanket Barbie
Maui Madness
Derby Divas
Haunted Hamlet
Turkeys, Tuxes, and Tabbies
Christmas Cozy
Alaskan Alliance
Matrimony Meltdown
Soul Surrender
Heavenly Honeymoon
Hopscotch Homicide
Ghostly Graveyard
Santa Sleuth

Zoe Donovan Cookbook

Ashton Falls Cozy Cookbook

Paradise Lake Mystery:

Pumpkins in Paradise
Snowmen in Paradise
Bikinis in Paradise
Christmas in Paradise
Puppies in Paradise
Halloween in Paradise

Whales and Tails Mystery:

Romeow and Juliet
The Mad Catter
Grimm's Furry Tail
Much Ado About Felines
The Legend of Tabby Hollow
The Cat of Christmas Past

Seacliff High Mystery:

The Secret
The Curse
The Relic
The Conspiracy
The Grudge

Road to Christmas Romance:

Road to Christmas Past

Chapter 1

Saturday, May 16

"Well, if it isn't my favorite passenger, Ms. Caitlin Hart," John Goodwin said as I drove the white panel van with the Harthaven Cat Sanctuary logo painted on the side onto the ferry just moments before it was due to pull away from the mainland and head toward Madrona Island. "Cutting it a bit close, aren't we?"

"I got held up at the adoption clinic and didn't realize what time it was until it was almost too late," I explained.

"So you had a good day?" John asked as he signaled the captain that they were clear to pull away.

"A very good day," I answered the weathered seaman through my open window. John had once owned his own fishing boat, but a mild stroke had caused him to settle into semiretirement as a part-time deckhand for the Washington State ferry system.

"I managed to find homes for all eight kittens I brought with me," I added, "and I squeezed in two follow-up visits for the adult pair I placed on my last trip. While I was there I also took possession of three short-timers from the kill shelter in town. I haven't had a lot of time with the new cats, but I think they'll all be adoptable once they get shots and health checks. You aren't perchance in the market for a cat?"

"Every time you make the trip to the mainland you try to talk me into adopting a cat," John pointed out.

"You can't blame a girl for trying." I grinned at the man, who was a good foot taller than my five-foot frame.

"Did you ever get your permit for the cats worked out with the county?" John wondered.

"Yeah. We were able to get a waiver, in spite of the fact that Mayor Bradley tried to get the sanctuary closed down. It was touch-and-go for a while, but in the end Maggie was able to convince the county that a cat sanctuary was a much better solution to the feral cat problem than extermination."

"I for one am glad it worked out. Hate to see all those kitties rounded up and sent off to kill shelters. Based on the number of cats I've seen running around, I imagine you have a full house."

"We do. Maggie rescued three additional pregnant females, and four of the females we've been housing have had kittens in the past couple of months. It's been pretty crowded, but as the kittens are adopted and the adults neutered and spayed, we hope to regain a level of control over the number of felines in residence."

"My grandson has been asking about a kitten for his birthday. I'll have a chat with his mother about the possibility."

"Thanks." I smiled at the tall, thin man with thinning white hair. "We have an easygoing orange tabby who would be perfect for a younger child. She's really mellow and loves to be held. She'll be old enough for a new home in a week, but we can keep her longer if you decide you need more time to get ready for her."

"I'll definitely let you know."

The wind began to pick up as the ferry left the protection afforded by the islands closest to the mainland and set off across the channel toward the westernmost island of Madrona. It really is beautiful in my corner of the world. The water is as blue as the sky and the endless miles of evergreen trees are so dense that it looks as if you could walk across the tops of them if you could get high enough. We don't have the variety of wildlife they have on the mainland, but what we have is abundant and awe-inspiring.

"Heard J pod is back," John said, referring to the resident orcas that hung out in the waters surrounding Madrona Island every summer.

"Yeah, they showed up a couple of days ago. The phone has been ringing off the hook at *Hart of the Sea*," I said. That's the whale-watching charter boat my brother Danny owns. "Given the sudden increase in reservations, I probably should have stayed behind to help Danny, but Maggie's still not back to her old self, so I didn't want her to make the trip into the city."

"Been a while," John commented.

"Yeah, although she seems a little better than she was. She's back to work at the Bait and Stitch part-time, though if you see her, don't mention the part-time. She keeps telling everyone she's back on her old full-time schedule, but most days she leaves early and lets Marley handle the lockup."

Marley Donnelly was Maggie's best friend and the co-owner of the Bait and Stitch, a unique shop that sold fishing supplies (Maggie's passion) and quilting supplies (Marley's obsession).

"Your aunt is a feisty old gal. I'm sure she'll be able to shake whatever nasty has a hold of her. If I know Maggie she won't stay down for long."

I laughed. "I hope so. I always figured it would be Maggie's strong opinions that led to her demise and not some stubborn flu. I'm helping her as much as I can. I try to take care of the cats and see to the cooking and whatnot, but she just seems so tired all the time. I'm really worried."

John buttoned the front of his jacket as the wind picked up. "Don't worry. Maggie is a firecracker who's been fueling the local gossip line her whole life. I'm sure when Maggie goes she'll make sure she goes out with a bang. She still talking about running for the island council?"

"She's turned in all the paperwork and is officially the front-runner of a very competitive campaign. I'm not sure the island can survive the name-calling that's been going back and forth between the four contenders for the only open seat. Personally, I can't wait . . . oh, crap." I slid down in my seat so I was completely hidden from view.

"Is there a problem?" John leaned in and looked at me through the open window.

"Of course there's a problem," I snapped. "I wouldn't be cowering under my dashboard if there wasn't a problem."

"Care to elaborate?" John raised one snowy white eyebrow.

"Do you see that man who just got out of the Mercedes at the front of the ferry?"

John pulled back a bit and looked toward the front of the vessel. "Dark hair, nice suit?"

"Is he coming this way?"

John turned and looked at me. "Nope. He took the stairs to the passenger deck."

I let out the breath I'd been holding and sat up slowly. I looked around just to be certain John hadn't been mistaken.

"I take it you're avoiding this man?" John asked as I tried to straighten the tie I'd wrapped around my unruly hair earlier in the day.

"His name is Camden Bradford. He's the new district manager at the bank."

"Are you behind on a loan?"

"No. It's just that Mr. Bradford happened to have a front-row seat to the most embarrassing moment of my life. I still wake up in a cold sweat from the nightmares I've suffered almost every night since it happened. I'm fairly certain I'll never be able to look the man in the eye again."

"Care to elaborate?"

I took a deep breath. I really didn't want to talk about my blunder, but I'd known John a long time and he certainly wasn't unaware of my tendency to get myself into embarrassing situations. Besides, he was a good listener and I really could use a sympathetic ear for the rant that had been building inside me for months.

Despite the fact that we were the only two passengers on the car deck, I sat up straight and leaned in close so I could lower my voice and still be heard. "When Maggie was in the hospital a few months ago things got tight financially. Really tight. She had a lot of testing done and the doctor bills were becoming a serious problem. I decided that the only solution was to go to the bank and ask for a short-term loan. Marley convinced me that the best shot I had at getting one was to let the girls do the talking."

"The girls?"

I blushed as I quickly glanced down at my breasts.

"Ah, the girls. Your aunt's business partner suggested that you use your breasts to get a loan?"

"Well, she didn't tell me I should sleep with the man, but she did suggest that I show up for my interview in a low-cut sweater. A *very* low-cut sweater. We both know how I tend to ramble on and on when I'm nervous, so we figured I'd have a better chance of success if I provided a distraction."

"And did it work?"

"It might have if Veronica hadn't popped out when I bent over to pick up the pen I'd dropped."

"Veronica?" John's blue eyes, faded with age, sparkled as he tried not to chuckle.

I glanced down at my chest and looked from the right to the left. "You know, Betty and Veronica."

"You call your breasts Betty and Veronica?"

"I didn't start it; Archie Longhorn did in the tenth grade, and I guess the names stuck."

John laughed out loud.

"It's not funny." I glared at him. "I've never been so humiliated in my life. I'm pretty sure that if Mr. Bradford comes back down to the car deck and heads in this direction I'm going to have to jump over the side and swim back to Madrona Island."

"What about the cats?"

"Oh, yeah. I forgot about the cats. I guess we'll just have to hope our local banker stays upstairs until I can make my getaway."

"You know, it might just be better to say hi to the man and get it over with."

"There's no way I'm going to say hi to the man. *Ever*."

"You can't avoid him indefinitely."

"Watch me."

"Madrona Island is a tight-knit community. Everyone runs into everyone else at some point," John said.

"Maybe, but Mr. Bradford doesn't live on Madrona, and he only spends time at the island branch on Mondays and Wednesdays. I've avoided him so far and I'm fairly confident in my ability to continue to do so."

"Today is Saturday," John pointed out.

I frowned. "It is Saturday. I wonder why he's coming to the island on a Saturday."

"Maybe he's decided to transfer to the island full-time."

"Don't even say that. If he transfers I'll have to move. If you see him coming warn me so I can duck back down."

"If he comes this way I'll divert him away from your van altogether," John promised.

"Thanks. You're a good friend."

I let out a sigh of relief and looked back toward the open channel. The water was calm, as it often was late in the day when there were few boats out and about. I loved the way the setting sun sparkled as it hit the water at just the right angle. It looked like little diamonds floating on the deep blue water.

"So did you get the loan after all that?" John asked after a bit.

"No. I took off after the incident and was too embarrassed to go back. Things turned out okay, though. Aiden worked out a discount with the doctor and Siobhan sent a check to cover what he couldn't negotiate." I referred to my oldest brother, who operates a fishing boat, and my sister, who lives in Seattle.

"Heard Aiden is headed to Alaska for the summer," John added.

"Yeah, he's chasing the fish." Aiden was the oldest of the Hart siblings and the heir to the family business. "A lot of folks think he should throw in the towel and sell his boat, but Aiden is the type who'll never give up in spite of the fact that the cannery has closed and many of the original fishing families have moved on."

"Fishing is a tough life, but for those of us who are born to it, it becomes part of our soul. If it weren't for my medical orders I'd be heading to Alaska myself this summer."

"It does seem like Aiden is only really happy when he's on the water," I admitted, "though I know Mom and Cassie really miss him when he's gone."

"Cassie still flunking math?" John asked about the youngest Hart sibling, who was sixteen years old.

"I've been working with her and I'm happy to say she's now the proud owner of a solid D plus. Sometimes I don't get her reluctance to do the work necessary for a respectable B, or even a C. She spends a lot of time socializing and playing games on her laptop, so I know she has a rudimentary knowledge of the machine, but when it comes time to dig into her homework she looks at it like it's a demon come to steal her soul."

"They do math on laptops now?"

"They do everything on laptops now," I informed him.

John shrugged. "Cassie is a smart girl. She'll figure it out."

"I hope so." I watched as the sun dipped beyond the horizon. Soon it would be dark, and with the darkness would come the cold. I loved the cabin I lived in on Maggie's property, overlooking the ocean, but it had been built as a summer home, so during the winter I had to be sure to keep a fire burning in the woodstove to ward off the chill.

"So are Maggie and Marley going to enter a float in the Founders Day parade this year?" John asked.

"They always enter one for the Bait and Stitch."

"Guess you heard that Francine is on the judging committee."

"Yeah, I heard." Francine Rivers was one of the contenders for the single seat on the island council, which had opened up when one of the members had announced he was going to retire. She also lived on the estate next to my aunt's. The two once had been good friends . . . until Maggie had built the cat sanctuary on the edge of her property. Not that Francine didn't like cats; she has a white Persian worth several thousand dollars named Juliet. The problem is that Francine doesn't want so many mangy strays—her words—near her cat show champion. She'd been trying to force Maggie to close or move the sanctuary ever since it opened.

"She's had quite a lot to say about her competition," John said. "I hope the fact that she's been going round and round with your aunt doesn't hurt her chances of getting a fair score."

"I'm sure Francine won't let her feud with my aunt interfere with what she thinks is best for the event."

Francine was a nice woman, and I personally got along well with her, but, like Aunt Maggie, she tended toward public displays of opinion.

"How are things going with your bookstore project?" John asked.

"It seems to be moving along, although it's still much too early to claim success. Still, Tara and I are hopeful that we can negotiate a deal. We're going to tour the facility on Monday to try to better assess what needs to be done."

My best friend Tara O'Brian and I have been trying to find funding to convert the old cannery, which has been empty since it closed down, into a coffee bar/bookstore/gathering spot that would not only provide a service to the community but also showcase the cats Maggie and I are trying to place in homes. Our idea was to convert the building into two spaces with an adjoining door. One side would house the coffee bar and bookstore. The second side would feature a lending library and reading room in which several hand-chosen cats would roam freely to interact with the general population. Madrona Island is a great place to live, but it's a small community that lacks a movie theater, bowling alley, night club, or other source of entertainment. The island residents needed a place to gather and socialize, and the old cannery was just sitting empty, without a purpose.

"I expect it's going to cost a small fortune to convert the space," John commented.

"It will, but Tara has applied for a loan, and a lot of our friends have offered to help out with free labor. I know we have a long way to go, but I'm really starting to get excited about the idea."

"Seems like a good project. Folks need a place to gather during the winter, when there isn't much going on. Have you come up with a name?"

"Coffee Cat Books."

John chuckled. "Clever. I like it. Have you addressed the issue of allowing the cats on the premises?"

"We have," I said proudly. "According to the board of health, as long as the cats aren't allowed in the area where food is prepared or sold, we don't have a problem. We plan to divide the space into two separate rooms joined by a glass wall and a glass door to provide a feeling of continuity, so we'll be fine."

"Sounds like you've thought it all out." John seemed impressed.

"The county has already approved our design and Danny drew up flyers that depict the concept we're going for."

"Can you e-mail me one?"

"Sure; let me get a pen." I dug around in my bottomless backpack for a pen and a pad of paper. I tend to be disorganized and forgetful at times, so the very organized Tara suggested that I start carrying around a pad and pen on which to take notes. The problem is that I can never find the pad and pen when I need them.

"Ah, here it is." I pulled the pad out of my purse. "Darn."

"Is there a problem?" John asked.

"I just noticed the note reminding me to get the flyers Maggie wants to hand out at the island council meeting printed while I was on the mainland."

"Flyers?" John asked.

"She put together some facts concerning Bill Powell's condo project and its potential impact on the community. The council is pretty much split down the middle on the controversy, and Maggie is hoping to negotiate a compromise."

"I'm afraid that isn't going to be an easy thing to negotiate. Those who want to maintain a quiet way of life on the island are at direct odds with those who're looking to modernize and bring in the tourist dollar. I know the condominium development is at the heart of the debate, but if you want my opinion, this controversy has been slowly creeping up on us for years."

"Yeah," I said, "I have to agree. It seems like the tensions among the island families really started back when the cannery closed and the ferry began to stop here. The ferry opened the door for folks from the mainland to visit Madrona Island for the weekend, which also opened the door for folks like Bill Powell to cash in by building condos folks can buy to use as vacation homes. I've tried to be impartial as I've listened to both sides of the debate, and to be honest, I'm not sure where I stand on the whole thing. I do know that no matter who wins, there's going to be discord among friends."

"Yup, I imagine there will be."

"It frightens me to think that the island could be divided to the point where families who once shared Sunday supper will no longer even speak to one another. It wasn't that long ago that the whole island would come out for community picnics in the park. When's the last time the whole community came together like that?"

"I guess it's been a while," John admitted. "Still, I've been around a long time, and in that time I've discovered one thing to be true: small towns are like family. They bicker and gossip, and at times go as far as to declare all-out war among members, but when push comes to shove, they'll always be there for you."

I sighed. "I hope you're right."

John squeezed my shoulder in a show of support. He knew how much I longed for the easy sense of community the island once knew.

"I'd better prepare the vessel for docking," John announced. "It looks like the passengers are starting to return to their cars. I doubt Mr. Bradford will come in this direction, but you might want to scrunch down a bit just in case he uses the back stairwell."

I laughed. "Thanks, John. You're a good friend. And let me know what you decide about the kitten."

I reached into the cooler behind me and grabbed a grape soda for the ride home. I'd brought a six pack but never had taken the time to enjoy one of the sweet and fizzy beverages. I watched as the ferry pulled toward the dock.

I loved Madrona Island. I'd lived there my entire life. I couldn't imagine living anywhere else, but the past few years have seen more change than the hundred before that. My great-great-grandfather was one of the twelve founding fathers who settled on the island. He worked hard, established a fishing empire, and raised seven children. One by one the founding families had died off or moved, and now very few of the original settlers remained. As John and I had discussed, those looking to maintain the way of life they'd always known had no use for the ferry, the tourists it brought, or the development that had followed. Others argued that now that the cannery had closed and commercial fishing in the area was all but dead, there was a need for a new source of revenue. Increased development, they argued, would bring jobs that would allow those who desired to do so to stay on the island, where their families had lived for generations.

I can understand both sides of the conflict. Like many members of the founding families, I have no desire to see condominiums rising up along the shore, destroying the natural beauty and solitude of the island. On the other hand, without the inflow of cash that tourism brings, most families couldn't afford to stay on the island and would be faced with moving altogether. It's a complicated issue that won't be decided overnight. I just hoped that while things were negotiated, the people I loved would be able to retain the friendships we've always known.

"Ms. Hart."

I heard a deep voice from just behind my window. I screamed, turned around, and tossed my soda directly into the man's smiling face.

Chapter 2

Monday, May 18

Monday morning dawned bright and sunny. I had a million and one things to see to but decided that the most important thing I needed to do was to take my dog, Max, for his morning run along the beach. There's something relaxing about running on the sand as the waves crash onto the shore and the thunder of the tide is the only sound that penetrates the rhythm of your own breath. It was a cool morning, so I'd bundled up in a heavy sweatshirt and long sweatpants before pulling a knitted cap over my long ponytail.

Max is a Border collie mix and my best friend in the world. I found him close to death after he'd been thrown from a boat when he was just a puppy. I'd nursed him back to health, and during the long hours I'd sat by his side and prayed that each breath wouldn't be his last, we'd forged a bond that few people really understand.

Max and I spend as much time together as we can. He's very well trained and often accompanies me when I go into town or make trips to the mainland, although since Maggie has been ill, I've been leaving him home when Maggie is going to be alone. Maggie's a cat person and not usually all that interested in dogs, but I know that if something were to happen while I was away, Max would go for help if Maggie was unable to get to a phone.

After Max and I had run along the beach for several miles I cut up to the road and turned onto the main highway so I could circle through the business district of Pelican Bay. Madrona Island is made up of two distinct villages: Harthaven Bay to the north, where I grew up and most of the longtime families still live, and Pelican Bay to the south. The community of Pelican Bay—I don't know why it's named that; there have never been any pelicans on the island—is a new development that sprang up when the ferry began to provide service to the island. While Harthaven Bay is a functional village with residential neighborhoods, a school, and practical stores such as a market, a drugstore, and a hardware store, Pelican Bay is a touristy type village, with art galleries, restaurants, B and Bs, and cute mom-and-pop shops, designed to meet the needs of our visitors.

As I neared the harbor I turned down the first row of residences, which paralleled the oceanfront road where most of Pelican Bay's businesses could be found.

"Good morning, Bella," I called, greeting one of the self-labeled witches who owned Herbalities, an interesting shop that sells herbal remedies and offers fortune-telling services. I'm not convinced that either Bella or her partner, Tansy, are *actual* witches, but you're unlikely to meet two nicer or more free-spirited women.

"Caitlin, how are you, dear?" Bella held a watering can and was providing moisture for a row of red vine roses that traveled over trellises at the front of her house.

"I'm good. Is Tansy doing better after her fall?"

Tansy had been hiking over the weekend when she'd stepped on some loose shell and tumbled down the side of the embankment.

"She's doing much better; thank you for asking. She has a few cuts and bruises, but it doesn't appear that she broke any bones. She's inside, mixing up some herbs to use as a salve to put on her scrapes. Would you like to come in for some tea?"

"I'd love to, but Max is wet from his romp through the waves and I really should get back to Maggie. I like to be home in time to make her breakfast before she leaves for the Bait and Stitch."

"Speaking of Maggie, I have some herbs for her to try." Bella swiped at one of the tendrils of long hair that had escaped the knot she'd formed on the top of her head. "It seems odd that her flu has lasted as long as it has. I'm hoping that an herb packet for overall vitality will put a spring back into her step."

"That's very nice of you. I'm sure she'll appreciate it. If you want to fetch it I'll take it to her so she can start on the herbs today. Max and I will just wait here since we're both wet and sandy," I offered.

"Nonsense." Bella bent down and petted Max behind the ears. "A little sand and seawater never hurt anyone. Come in and have one of the muffins Tansy made for you this morning. You can take some to Maggie as well."

"Tansy made me muffins?"

"Boysenberry, your favorite."

"But I never told Tansy I planned to stop by. In fact, I hadn't planned to stop by at all. I was just running down the street and saw you in the yard."

Bella just smiled as she picked up her watering can and started back to the house. "Did the cat adoption go well?"

"Really well," I said as Max and I followed Bella up the walkway toward the cute little house she and Tansy shared. The house reminded me of a Cape Cod style with its slanted roof and dormer windows. The cottage itself was white with black shutters and a large covered porch overlooked the sea in the distance. "I managed to place all the cats I brought with me, including Hercules."

Hercules was a large stripped tabby Bella had found and brought to Harthaven over the winter.

"I think he's going to be very happy," I added. "The woman who adopted him had a wide lap for sitting and a pocket full of salmon treats all ready to dish out. She's retired and lives alone, so I predict the two will be a great pair."

"I have no doubt that Hercules will have a very good life with Emma."

I frowned. I'd never mentioned the woman's name. It sort of freaked me out when Bella and Tansy did things like that. You'd think I'd be used to it by now, but somehow chatting with someone who knew more about your life than you did was a bit unnerving.

"Go ahead and have a seat while I put on some tea," Bella offered. I sat down at the large table I knew had been formed from a piece of a ship's hull. Like most of the rooms in the home, the kitchen was accented with items from the island and the surrounding sea.

"Have you painted since the last time I was here?" I asked. The interior of the home was bright with an abundance of natural light from the large windows that had been added to the rear of the house, but the walls seemed a lighter shade of the yellow than I remembered.

"Tansy felt we needed a facelift. She said she sensed a dark aura after those tourists vandalized the place a few months ago. I'm not sure how well fresh paint can deal with the negative energy left behind by such an experience, but I like the color."

I smiled. "I like it as well."

Bella set a cup of tea and a freshly made muffin in front of me.

"Go ahead and get started," she instructed. "I'll just run upstairs and get Tansy."

"No need to bother her—" I began.

"Nonsense. It will brighten her day to visit with you and Max."

Max had lain down on the floor while I nibbled on my muffin. At first glance Bella and Tansy's place looked like any other house. There were cast-iron pots hanging from a rack, a bouquet of fresh flowers graced the table, a basket of fresh fruit sat on the tile counter, bunches of dried herbs hung from the ceiling, and healthy green potted plants had been set on several surfaces. Upon closer examination, however, visitors realized that the plants growing in the enclosed sunporch to the rear of the house were actually herbs, and the knickknacks placed around the room were talismans strategically placed for specific purposes.

"Good morning, Agatha," I greeted the pure black cat Maggie had placed with Bella and Tansy over a year ago. She purred and wrapped herself around my legs as we both waited for Bella to reappear.

There was something serene about sitting in Bella and Tansy's kitchen. I'm not sure I can describe the feeling exactly, but the room seemed to embrace you with its warmth. It most likely had to do with the sweet-smelling herbs, softly ringing wind chimes, and abundance of natural light that filtered in at just the right angle.

"Cait, I'm so glad you stopped by." Tansy, dressed in a long peasant skirt and a white blouse, with her feet bare, swept into the room with such grace that you'd never know she'd taken a fall. "I made you some of your favorite muffins."

"They're delicious, but how did you know I'd stop by?" I asked the petite and fair-skinned woman with jet-black hair that hung to her waist. "Even I didn't know I was going to until I did."

"I had a hunch."

"I'm glad to see you're doing well after your fall," I offered.

"Right as rain." Tansy handed me a paper bag of muffins that she must have already packed before I arrived. "Be sure that Maggie takes the herbs Bella went to fetch and eats one of these muffins before she heads out for the day."

"Okay, I'll give them to her," I promised as tall and slim, blond-haired and blue-eyed Bella handed me the packet of herbs.

"Now finish up your tea," Tansy instructed. "As much as I'd like to sit and chat, you really should get going. We wouldn't want to keep Romeo waiting."

"Romeo?"

Tansy smiled but didn't elaborate.

I stood up and gathered my things. I should know by now that Tansy never really told you anything but preferred to hint at things that for some reason only she knew.

"Thank you for the muffins and the herbs." I picked up the bags and motioned for Max to join me.

I said my good-byes to Bella, who had wandered back outside to finish the watering while I was speaking to Tansy, and then continued down the road toward the land where my cabin resided at Whale Watch Point. Maggie had inherited the estate from her mother, who inherited it from her grandfather. It really was a beautiful piece of property, located on the edge of a peninsula that looked toward Canada to the north. The peninsula was originally developed by three of the families that settled on the island more than a hundred years before.

Maggie's property was in the center third of the peninsula. Based on the shape of the peninsula and the dense forest covering most of the land mass, you can stand almost anywhere and not see the structures on the other two properties. Maggie's house was set back on the center of the huge lot, while my cabin sat within a few feet of the water to the left. The building that housed the cats was all the way to the right, bordering the property owned by Francine Rivers.

As I mentioned before, the fact that Maggie had built the cat sanctuary so close to Francine and her expensive show cat had caused a rift between two women who had grown up as best friends.

As Max and I turned from the main road onto the narrow lane that serviced the homes on the peninsula, I noticed a large gray cat trotting along behind us. I stopped and turned to consider the long-haired animal. "Romeo?" I said.

The cat just looked at me, neither running away nor coming closer. I realized this was who Tansy had referred to, so I turned and continued down the lane. Once I'd reached Maggie's property Romeo sprinted the remaining distance toward my front deck, where he leaped into the swing and seemed to settle in for a nap.

Max trotted over and tried to greet our guest with a sniff, but Romeo just hissed. I opened the front door of my cabin and invited him inside, but he lazily opened one eye, then began to purr as he drifted off to kitty dreamland.

"I think we might have a new roommate," I told Max as I filled his food and water dishes and put coffee on to perk.

Max just wagged his tail as I left him to his breakfast. I wandered into my small bathroom to shower and prepare for the day. The cabin Max and I share is little more than a studio. There's a large loft upstairs, which I use as a bedroom. It has an A-frame shape so that the center of the room has a higher ceiling than either side. There's plenty of room for a queen-size bed, a small closet, a dresser, a desk, and a chair. The bed is situated so that I can wake up every morning to the sight of the ocean just outside my window. Although the room is small, I've built bookshelves into every wall except the one with the window. I love the feeling of waking up to so many possibilities.

Downstairs there's a small but functional kitchen that's open to a seating area that features two large, overstuffed sofas arranged in front of a small brick fireplace so that the view of the ocean is unobstructed. There's a dining table and chairs in front of the window that overlooks the green forest to the back of the property.

After showering and dressing I made a couple of eggs and some toast, then went out front to check on Romeo. When I opened the door he looked up, jumped down from the swing, and trotted inside. I knew I should take him to the cat sanctuary, but somehow I realized that, for the time being at least, Romeo and I were meant to spend some quality time together.

"Stay off the dining table and the kitchen counters and we'll get along fine," I promised the huge tomcat.

Romeo simply wound a figure 8 through my legs.

"I'm not sure how long you'll be staying with Max and me, but we welcome you and hope your stay is pleasant. The resident cats are allowed out onto the property during the day when Aunt Maggie and I are home to keep an eye on things, but there are two rules you must obey: Don't leave the property and please, please stay away from the white Persian next door."

Romeo glanced up and looked at me as if he understood. I certainly hoped he did. Maggie and I take our guardianship of the felines on the island very seriously. It's not only unwise for them to venture from the estate but dangerous as well. When Mayor Bradley lost several expensive koi from his pond to the feral cats that populate the island, he railroaded the island council into passing a law making it legal to round up cats that wandered onto your property and destroy them, or drop them off at the kill shelter on the mainland. Unfortunately, there were some who'd decided to make a sport out of these cat hunts. That was when Maggie decided to open the Harthaven Cat Sanctuary, offering no-questions-asked housing for any and all cats that were dropped off. While most residents of the island were glad for a no-kill solution to the wild cat population that had spiraled out of control, there were a few old geezers who took unusual joy in hunting the cats that had the misfortune of wandering onto their property.

"If you can do those two things you'll be given the run of the property. If not, I'm afraid you'll be required to spend your time with us in one of the cat rooms. Don't worry; if that should occur, the rooms are very comfortable. Each one has soft bedding, an indoor and outdoor play area, and other cats to hang out with."

Romeo just stared at me as I rambled on. Did I mention that I tend to ramble? I had a litter box and some dry cat food from a prior visitor, so I got Romeo set up on the closed-in back porch before Max and I set off for town and the meeting that could very well change the course of our lives.

Chapter 3

The old cannery that Tara and I hoped to convert was located at the end of the wharf, near the dock where the ferry loaded and unloaded. I glanced inside through the dirty window as I waited for Tara to arrive. The building was large, and once remodeled it would serve Tara and me and the people of the community quite well.

"Sorry I'm late. Keith Weaver, the Realtor I was supposed to meet, never showed up, even though I waited at his office for over half an hour. I called the bank and was told it was okay for us to go ahead and check out the building ourselves."

"Do you have a key?" I asked.

"There's a lockbox. I have the combination." Tara and I walked toward the entry. Tara had started to type in the combo she'd been provided with when I noticed the door was open.

"Don't bother," I told her. "It looks like the last person out forgot to lock the door."

Tara frowned and then shrugged. She opened the door and stepped inside.

It was an excellent location, but it really did need a *lot* of work. There was dirt and dust covering everything, and several of the windows were cracked.

I bent over and picked up a yellow flyer someone had left on the floor. "It looks like Bill Powell is having a seminar on his new condos this evening, if you're in the market for a new residence," I joked. "It says there'll be doughnuts and coffee."

"Thanks but no thanks," Tara emphasized. "The project he has planned is so commercial. It's going to stand out like a sore thumb on the island."

I wadded up the flyer and tossed it on the floor. Normally I'm not one to litter, but one more piece of paper in a sea of debris wasn't going to make much difference. "It seems a bit ballsy for Powell to have a seminar to market the condos when his project has yet to be approved by the island council."

"Yeah, well, Bill is a ballsy sort of guy, but I heard Keith Weaver has partnered up with him to get the project approved at the next council meeting."

I paused. "Really? I thought Keith was worried about the effect of the condos on the island's water supply."

Tara shrugged. "He was, but I guess Powell got to him. I chatted with Kim for a bit while I waited for Keith to show up this morning. She said he's demonstrated a complete change of heart."

I knew Kim Darby worked in Keith Weaver's real estate office. If Keith had teamed up with Bill, Kim could very well have overheard their conversation.

"I'm surprised Maggie hasn't said anything. If Powell can swing Keith's vote the project might actually get approved."

"Maybe she doesn't know. The men seem to have been keeping their alliance quiet. I think they plan to spring it on everyone at the next meeting."

"I really need to tell her. This is something she'll want to prepare for. Remind me to call her when we're done here."

Tara took a notepad and pencil from her shoulder bag. I noticed she didn't have to fish around or dump out her bag to find the items she was looking for, as I always seemed to need to. Of course, Tara has been a list maker since birth, while I'm a newbie to the art. The thing is, Tara and I are different. She likes to approach a project in a very methodical manner. Me, I'm fine with looking around and making a decision based on a glance. Now my glance confirmed what I already knew: the building would be perfect for Coffee Cat

Books. I was good to go, but I knew that once Tara took out her notepad we'd be there for a while.

"We need to measure the walls on these two sides," she announced. "Hold the tape measure so I can get an accurate distance between the storage room and the space where we plan to put the seating area."

I held the tape measure while Tara measured and remeasured several times. Each time she completed a measurement she'd jot down a note in her little book.

"I thought we could put the wall to divide the two areas about here." She indicated a location in the large room. "We can put the coffee bar on that wall and then put tables and chairs roughly in front of it." She turned and considered the rest of the space. "I want to have a cute display near the entrance from the wharf, and then we can build shelves in this larger space." She waved her arm in a sweeping gesture.

"And the cat lounge?"

Tara walked to the far end of the building, which hung out over the water.

"We'll set up sofas near the old stone fireplace and comfortable chairs in the center of the room. This will be a good area to glass off and use as a reading room," Tara commented as I followed her around. "Chances are people will strike up conversations in the less formal seating area, so those who want quiet to study can sit at one of the individual tables in the reading room."

Tara walked across the space toward the far wall. "I think we should replace all of this siding with windows looking out into the harbor."

The view really was spectacular. To the east was the marina, filled with boats both large and small, and to the west was unobstructed shoreline.

"Are you sure we can afford this?" I asked as Max trotted over to sniff at whatever had scurried under a long counter, which, like the rest of the building, was in pretty bad shape.

"It's going to be tight," she admitted. "And we'll need to get the full amount of the loan I applied for, but I've gone over the numbers and I think we can make it work. The terms of the purchase of the property are reasonable, but there's one small problem."

"Problem?" I asked as I watched the ferry pull in across the way.

"We need to not only fill out the loan application but complete an interview with a representative from the district office."

"Not Camden Bradford?"

"I'm afraid so."

"There's no way I'm going to have a meeting with Camden Bradford. You know what happened last time."

"I do." Tara sighed. She walked across the room in her pink and purple flip-flops and looped her arm through mine. "I know that you were embarrassed by what happened, but it was several months ago and I doubt he remembers."

"Oh, he remembers all right."

"How do you know? He's a busy man with a lot of contacts."

I leaned against the window. The room was filled with old equipment but not a single place to sit. "I ran into Mr. Bradford on the ferry," I said.

"Really? When?"

"Saturday. I was going to tell you about it, but this is the first time I've seen you since it happened."

"Tell me exactly what happened."

I turned so that I was looking out the window and my back was to Tara. "He snuck up on me from behind. I was already jittery because I'd seen him earlier, and when he stuck his head into the van and said hi I screamed and dumped my soda all over the front of his very expensive white shirt. It was grape soda. I'm sure he had to throw the shirt away."

"Oh, Cait, you didn't." Tara groaned.

"'Fraid so."

"Was he mad?"

I thought about it. "Actually, he was surprisingly not mad. He laughed and apologized for sneaking up on me."

"And then?"

"And then the ferry docked, and he told me that next time he would make more noise if he was going to approach me from behind. He even suggested that he might take up whistling when I was in the area. Then he went to his car, which, by the way, probably cost more than a bank manager makes in a year. You don't think maybe he launders money for the mob, do you?"

"Launders money for the mob? You've been watching too many movies."

"He has a Mercedes that must have set him back a pretty penny. At the time I was so freaked out about running into him that I didn't think about the fact that it made no sense that he could afford a car like that. If he isn't laundering money, maybe he deals drugs or works for a hit man."

"Don't be ridiculous," Tara snapped. "He might have family money, or maybe he won the lottery or has a rich wife. I doubt he's a thug."

Tara bit the nail on her left thumb, a nervous habit she'd had since we were in preschool. I could tell she was annoyed with me, and to be honest, I didn't blame her. I'd probably ruined any chance we had of buying our dream location because I couldn't control my tendency toward skittishness.

"Maybe we can meet with someone assigned to the island branch," I suggested. The bank on the island is small, with just three full-time employees, none of whom I'd humiliated myself in front of.

"It's going to take approval from the main office for a loan the size we need," Tara countered.

"Maybe you can see Bradford alone," I proposed.

"The woman I spoke to specifically asked that we both be there. I'm sure we both need to go over the terms, and we both have to sign the loan documents."

I sighed. "Okay."

Tara hugged me. "Don't worry; it'll be fine. We have an appointment at three. I need to do," Tara looked at her notebook, switched to another page, and counted, "seven errands before our meeting. Each one shouldn't take more than twenty minutes. Why don't you plan to meet me in front of the bank at 2:45?"

"Yeah, okay."

"And Cait . . . no low-cut tops and no open cans of soda."

I was about to make a joke about both when I noticed that Max had left the room while we'd been talking. "Max," I called.

He barked from somewhere in the distance. The only other room was the enclosed area at the end of the building, which had been used for storage. That was where we planned to build an office and locate the litter boxes for the cats. There were no windows in that room, which made it dark. There was an overhead light, but the electricity was turned off. I slowly entered the dark and dusty room that still held boxes of someone's stuff.

"Max," I called again. He whimpered but didn't move. I walked across the space to see what he'd been so mesmerized by. Someone probably had left garbage for my dog to find, which wasn't going to make me happy at all. The last time he'd gotten into a garbage can he'd puked all night. I was still trying to get the smell out of the carpet.

I jumped as I bumped into something, which turned out to be an abandoned piece of machinery. I was about to turn around when I remembered that my phone had a flashlight. I pulled it from my pocket and turned it on. The room really was a mess.

"What did you find?" I asked as I peered over Max's furry shoulder.

Max looked up just about the time I let out a bloodcurdling scream.

Chapter 4

"And you said the door was open when you arrived?" Deputy Ryan Finnegan—Finn to his friends—asked us. Finn was the resident deputy on Madrona Island and my older sister Siobhan's ex-fiancé. When Siobhan was offered a job in Seattle she'd broken her promise to Finn and headed east without a second thought. I knew for a fact that Siobhan had moved on, but at times I wasn't certain Finn ever would.

"Yes, the door was unlocked," I answered. "Tara had the code to get into the lockbox where the key was stored, but I noticed the door was ajar before she even finished putting it in. We figured the last person to access the property had probably forgotten to lock up."

Finn walked across the room to the front door, where the lockbox was located, and, using a rag so as not to leave any fingerprints, removed the key. "Did either of you touch the key?" he asked.

Tara and I both said we hadn't.

"It's a long shot, but I might be able to get a print off the key or the box. So, you arrived and began to look around. What made you decide to go into the back room where Mr. Weaver's body was found?"

"Max wandered into the room and found the body," I answered. "If he hadn't gone sniffing around, we most likely would have left without ever finding the body. How long do you think he's been dead?"

"I'll need to wait for the medical examiner to arrive from the mainland, but I'm going to guess around twelve hours. Did either of you see anyone else in the area when you arrived?"

I looked at Tara.

"I didn't," she said.

"Yeah, me neither."

"Okay. I'll need you to walk me through your movements from the moment you got here until I arrived."

Tara and I filled Finn in the best we could. Finn is a good guy, and I was sure he'd get to the bottom of Keith Weaver's murder. Sometimes I find myself mourning the fact that he'll never be an official part of our family. I know he was devastated when Siobhan left the island, and as strange as this may sound, I'm fairly certain I took Siobhan's breakup with Finn harder than she did. They'd dated since their sophomore year of high school, and he'd been a daily part of our lives for a lot of years. In many ways he was like a brother to me.

"If one of the deputies from the main office comes around to investigate, it's important that you stick to the facts and only answer what's asked," Finn cautioned me. He knows I tend to ramble, and I'm sure he doesn't want the woman who is akin to a little sister to him behind bars for saying the wrong thing to the wrong person.

"I'll let Tara do all the talking," I said.

Finn seemed satisfied with that response.

When Finn told us we were free to go I headed home to drop off Max and check on Romeo. I really wasn't looking forward to my meeting with Camden Bradford, but I'd promised Tara I'd be there and so I would. I knew Tara's schedule was going to be off, which would toss her into a bit of a frenzy, but I also knew she'd show up at the bank looking cool, calm, and collected. Tara was one of those unique individuals who always seemed to know what needed to be done and exactly how to do it.

"How was your morning in your new home?" I picked up Romeo and gave him a warm cuddle. The large cat began to purr as I rubbed my cheek against his soft fur. "I'm afraid I'm going to have to leave you again, but we'll try spending some time outdoors when I get back."

Romeo dug his head into my neck as I scratched his back. I doubt he'd been on the street long to be this affectionate. He buried his head under my thick, long hair as I hugged him one final time before setting him on the floor. I checked his food and water, topped off Max's water, grabbed my backpack, and headed out the door.

It was a nice day and I was tempted to ride my bike into Pelican Bay, but I hated to show up all sweaty. On the other hand, I didn't want to waste even one minute of sunshine, so the bike won out over my twenty-year-old car.

The ride along the seashore was breathtaking. There was a dirt path that hugged the coastline all the way to the harbor. Once I reached the wharf I headed to the far end, where the one and only bank that served the island was located. I wished I could say I felt brave and confident as I locked up my two-wheeled, human-propelled mode of transportation, but the truth of the matter was, I was terrified. I walked slowly along the boardwalk toward the entrance, where I had arranged to meet Tara. I know this is going to sound crazy, but I felt like a prisoner on her way to execution, as if the long walk up the wooden walkway would be my last.

"Ready?" Tara, dressed in a bright sundress topped with a practical cardigan, asked.

"Not really. In fact, I'm pretty sure I'm going to lose the lunch I didn't have in the hedge."

"It'll be fine," Tara assured me. "I'll do the talking. You just need to sit there and look beautiful. Although," Tara looked me up and down, "you might have driven so you would have avoided the inevitable dusty shin syndrome you get when you ride on that old dirt trail."

I looked down. Tara was right; from my knees down, my legs were covered with a thin layer of silt. "It was such a nice day," I explained.

Tara wiped cat hair from the shoulder of my blouse. My clothes are always covered in cat hair—an occupational hazard from running a cat sanctuary, I suppose.

"Run this through your hair." Tara handed me a brush.

I did as instructed and then turned around for inspection. "Better?"

"Marginally." She looked me over, biting her lip, as if trying to decide if there was anything else to be done. "What's wrong with your neck?"

I scratched the right side just under my ear. "Just a little itch. It'll be fine. Let's get this over with."

Luckily, Mr. Bradford didn't keep us waiting. We were shown into his office and instructed to take seats across from his desk. I tried to make my way across the room, sit down where I was told, and avoid tripping, all while never looking up or making eye contact of any type.

"Ms. O'Brian, Ms. Hart, thank you for coming in today," Mr. Bradford began. "I wasn't certain you'd make it after the incident this morning."

"There didn't seem to be any more we could do at this point," Tara said. "I imagine you've been interviewed by the sheriff's office?"

"I just finished up with them. The building has been cordoned off for now, but I've been assured that once the investigation has been completed I'll be free to sell the space as planned. My question to you now is whether you're still interested."

"We are," Tara answered for both of us. "Did the sheriff give you an idea of when they might complete their investigation?"

"He wouldn't say. I suppose it depends on how long it takes to figure out who killed the guy."

"I understand. We're still interested," Tara repeated.

"Very well, then. Let's discuss the funding you propose."

I tuned out while Tara droned on about the estimated cost to complete the remodel and the projected cost to maintain the facility once it opened. I'd always been good in math and had helped to develop the projections, but I have a curious mind that's easily distracted and tends not to want to focus on any one thing for too long.

The warmer weather served as a reminder of the busy summer season that was just around the corner. Living on the island was like living in two completely different cultures at the same time. During the off-season, which spanned October through May, there were very few visitors, and many of the touristy type shops on the island shut down for the season. I enjoyed that time of the year, when the pace was slower and good friends could gather for a meal and not have to compete with guests from the mainland for a table near the window of restaurants.

And then there was the summer season, when the population of the island nearly tripled on the weekends. Businesses that had been closed since October began to open and seasonal workers began to arrive. With the arrival of the masses came a certain energy that felt akin to the island coming to life after a long and peaceful hibernation. Most years by the end of the summer I was ready for the slower pace of winter, and likewise, most winters when spring arrived I was ready for the energy of summer.

Tara nudged my leg, which brought me back to the conversation going on around me. "I guess that's true," she was admitting. "Might I ask . . ."

Tara's words were cut off by the ringing of the phone on Mr. Bradford's desk.

"I'm sorry; I really need to take this," Bradford said.

"Certainly. No problem," Tara assured him.

I sat up a bit straighter while the man was otherwise occupied and looked out the window toward the blue water and white sails in the harbor. It really was a beautiful day. I was about to say as much when Tara kicked the side of my leg, harder this time.

I glanced at her.

She gave me a look that let me know she wasn't happy with me.

"What?" I mouthed without making a sound.

"Stop scratching," she mouthed back.

Suddenly I realized that I'd been scratching the entire time we'd been in the office. I looked down at my arms, which were red with welts from my nails.

"Dammit," I said aloud just as Mr. Bradford hung up.

"Is there a problem?" he asked.

"No, not at all," I lied, though it was apparent to me that my little Romeo had fleas that he'd kindly transferred to me when I'd cuddled with him before coming into town.

"You were saying?" Mr. Bradford asked Tara as I used every ounce of willpower I possessed to sit still and not scratch.

"I wanted to ask about the timeline for the loan approval process," Tara answered. "I've already begun lining up contractors so we can get started as soon as the money is available."

"Once everything is in order loan approval should only take a few days. I like what I see; however, I'd like the two of you to rework your proposal so that the concerns I've outlined are addressed. Now that the building is quarantined and we're in a waiting pattern, the urgency to get the space sold has lessened considerably."

I began to squirm around in my chair.

"Is everything okay?" Mr. Bradford asked me.

"Everything is perfect." I smiled in return.

"I'd like to set up another meeting to discuss your ideas further once you've had the chance to think about the things we've discussed today."

"That's acceptable to me. Caitlin?" Tara turned to look at me. I was scratching like crazy by this point. She pleaded with her eyes for me to get it under control.

I jumped up. "I have to go. I'll talk to you later," I said to Tara as I ran out the office door and out of the building. I simply couldn't sit there one more minute while the tiny aliens that had invaded my body snacked on my flesh.

The thought of riding all the way home with the fleas nipping at my skin was more than I could take, so I slipped off my shoes and dove into the harbor. I submerged myself until I was certain the little buggers that had been biting me had drowned. When I resurfaced I looked back toward the building I had just escaped. Mr. Bradford and Tara were looking out the window. Apparently, Caitlin Hart had managed to make another memorable impression.

Chapter 5

Tara and I are closet foodies. Every Monday evening, no matter what else might be going on, we meet at my cabin to watch our favorite show, *Cooking With Cathy*. And we don't just watch the show; we participate in the project of the evening. The really awesome thing about this specific cooking show is that the recipe and ingredients are provided online ahead of time, so you can prepare the dish right along with Cathy. This week, due to my unfortunate run-in with the fleas Romeo had felt inclined to share, I was staying in Maggie's guest room while my cabin was fumigated, so we were cooking in Maggie's much larger kitchen. I'd treated Romeo with flea powder I'd gotten from the vet when I returned from the bank, so he was sitting with Max and watching us as we made beefy enchiladas with a spicy red sauce.

"This looks almost as good as the seafood lasagna we made a few weeks ago," Tara commented as she began shredding the beef we'd cooked the day before in preparation for this evening's demonstration. "I made a whole batch of the lasagna the other day and I'm afraid I ate the entire thing all by myself."

"I thought you wanted to go on a diet before summer," I said.

"I do. I will. I just haven't started yet."

Tara is absolutely gorgeous, but she tends to carry a few extra pounds due, I imagine, to both her love of eating *and* her aversion to getting dirty and sweaty. I've tried several times to convince her to join Max and me on our runs, but she seems to always have an excuse to avoid doing so.

"I was thinking of joining that new exercise class they have at the community center on Tuesday and Thursday mornings."

Tara hesitated.

"You know you want to get into that red dress for your cousin's wedding," I reminded her.

"That's true. I guess I could work out two mornings a week."

"Great. I'll pick you up on my way." She'd be less likely to cancel if I showed up on her front step. "The class starts tomorrow, so I'll see you at eight."

"Eight?" Tara said weakly as she measured the red sauce into a measuring cup. "Maybe I should start next week."

"Two months, twenty pounds. Do the math."

"Okay." Tara sighed. "I'll be ready. Maybe we can get lattes on the way."

"Sure, if they're nonfat."

Tara looked at me as I grated the cheddar cheese. "How come we eat the same thing but you're so skinny?"

"Because I ride my bike into town on nice days even if I'll be dusty, and I run on the beach with Max even if my floors get sandy."

In addition to being obsessively organized, Tara is a neat freak who really does believe that cleanliness is next to godliness.

"I guess you have a point," Tara admitted. "How much sour cream are we supposed to use?"

"A cup and a half."

"It's too bad Maggie went up to bed so early," Tara added. "She loves enchiladas."

"I'm really worried about her," I said. "I feel like the progress she made last month is slipping away. Should we add the chilies to the tortillas or the sauce?"

"The tortillas."

"So how did things go after I left the bank?" I asked. "Did I totally blow any chance we had at getting a loan?"

Tara walked over to preheat the oven. "Quite the contrary. Mr. Bradford almost seemed," Tara paused as she searched for the right word, "charmed."

"Charmed? Are you kidding me? I fled his office and jumped in the harbor while he looked on. What's charming about that?"

Tara shrugged. "You got me. I was mortified, but he actually smiled. When I left he said he was looking forward to reviewing our reworked proposal."

"So you're saying that my tendency to be a total mess is actually working in our favor?"

"Oddly enough, it would seem it might be."

"Thanks for helping me," I said an hour later after our enchiladas were assembled and the show was over. Tara had offered to help me see to the cats in the sanctuary, which I needed to do twice a day.

"What are we going to do with those wonderful-looking enchiladas?" Tara asked. "There's no way I'm going to bust my butt exercising and then ruin it by eating any of the cheesy delights we just made."

"I thought I'd see if I could entice Maggie to eat a couple, and then I was going to divide what was left between Mr. Parsons and Mrs. Trexler."

Mr. Parsons was my reclusive next-door neighbor and Mrs. Trexler was my third-grade teacher who now lived alone and rarely got out since she lost her driver's license for running into the back of Finn's sheriff's vehicle. Twice.

"That's a good idea. I'm sure they'll both appreciate the gesture. In fact, maybe we should start taking part of the food we make every Monday to those in need. I love to watch Cathy's show, but she certainly doesn't pick low-calorie options."

"No, she doesn't." I laughed. "Last week's cheesecake had enough calories in it to feed a small town for a week. I've actually been taking my half of the food we make to Mrs. Trexler and Mr. Parsons for a while. From now on I'll just divide the entire serving."

I entered the first cat room, reserved for moms with kittens, and began the process of providing food and water, as well as clean linens and cat box litter. Each cat room has both an indoor and an enclosed outdoor area where the cats can lie in the sun, climb trees, and romp to their hearts' delight.

I picked up one of the resident kittens and cuddled it. Maggie made sure that all of the kittens born at the facility were given large doses of human interaction. Once they turned eight weeks of age they were spayed or neutered, given shots, and adopted by new families. The mama cats who could be rehabilitated were likewise altered and then adopted into forever homes.

"How many cats do you currently have in residence?" Tara wondered.

"Thirty-eight. Four mama cats, eighteen kittens, seven altered feral adults who have been given sanctuary in permanent quarters, and five altered males who we're working on finding homes for, as well as four altered females who show a lot of promise."

"That's a lot. What are you going to do if you get filled to capacity?"

"I try not to think about that. Six of the kittens are almost ready for new homes. I've had success with the adoption clinics in the city and I know that once the residents of Madrona Island start hanging out with the cats at Coffee Cat Books they'll want to adopt the cats they have a chance to meet. We've been aggressively altering the cats who come in, which will reduce the number of kittens born in the future."

"What about those you aren't able to rehabilitate?"

I bent down and picked up a huge orange tabby. "This is Moose. When we first trapped him and brought him here you couldn't get within ten feet of him, but now he comes over to say hi when I come in. He isn't quite ready for a home—he tends to scratch and bite if he's had enough people time—but I have hope that one day we'll find the perfect forever home for even him."

"And what about Romeo? Do you think he's here to stay?"

I thought about it. He seemed perfectly at home, but my intuition told me that he was only in my life for a visit.

"I guess we'll have to wait and see. Akasha didn't seem too thrilled to have another cat in the house."

Akasha was my aunt's cat, her first rescue. She's a dainty black beauty who adores my aunt but only tolerates everyone else. When Maggie had gone up to bed Akasha had gone with her.

Tara bent down and picked up a multicolored kitten who appeared to be some sort of Maine coon mix. "This little guy sure is friendly. Do you have a home for him yet?"

"Not yet," I said. "He seems to like you."

"I have to admit I'm tempted. Living alone can get lonely at times, and a cat would provide company. Have you named him?"

"No. I always leave that up to the forever families of the cats and kittens I feel are candidates for placement. Some of our resident feral cats have names."

Tara continued to hold the long-haired kitten with bright blue eyes. She turned him so they were face to face. "Aren't you a cutie? Do you shed a lot?" The kitten began to purr as it swatted her on the nose. "I bet you do shed a lot, but you're quite the charmer." Tara smiled as she rubbed her cheek against his soft fur.

I smiled too. It looked like Tara was going home with a cat. Maybe not today, but soon. I'm convinced that cats have a way of knowing who they should be with. Tara had helped me with the cats before and had stopped to pet the kittens each time but really hadn't shown a lot of interest in taking one home. Until today. Today the little bandit trotted over, stole a heart, and charmed his way into a forever home.

I walked over to the window and looked out as a car pulled into the drive. "Looks like Danny's here," I announced.

Tara immediately set the kitten down and began to straighten her hair. I suspect she has a crush on Danny. At first I found the attraction odd, but Danny *is* fun and spontaneous, with a joy for life that I seldom see in anyone over the age of puberty. I can see how Tara and Danny would be good for each other. She needs to lighten up a bit and he needs to take things a bit more seriously.

Danny must have noticed that the exterior lights of the sanctuary were on because he headed our way

"Hey, sis." Danny bent over and kissed me on the cheek. Then he turned and kissed Tara on the cheek as well.

"So what brings you to my neck of the woods this evening?" I asked.

Danny lived on his boat in the marina and was most often found at the pub nearby at this time of day.

"I was at O'Malley's tossing down a pint and you'll never guess who I ran into."

"Santa Claus."

"What? Why would you guess that?"

"You said I'd never guess, so I tried to imagine the least likely answer."

"I didn't run into Santa Claus, but I did run into Cody West."

I paled. Cody West was the boy who'd taken my virginity and then disappeared into the sunset, never to be seen or heard from again. Okay, maybe that's not exactly what happened. Exactly what happened was that I was foolish enough to fall in love with Danny's best friend, a boy two years my senior. According to both Danny and Tara, the only two people in the world who know the details of the series of events leading up to my still beating heart being ripped from my chest, the incident, at least in part, had been my fault.

Cody had been eighteen and a high-school senior, while I was sixteen and a sophomore. I'd been lusting after him since the moment I hit puberty, which most likely had led to my ill-advised plan. I managed to sneak into the party the senior class was having on graduation night, where I fully intended to seduce the guy I knew in my heart I was destined to spend the rest of my life with. On the surface it seemed that my seduction worked fantastically. While Cody tried to divert my attention in the beginning, I was persistent and managed to squeeze my way past his defenses. It was a magical night, a night of romance and intimacy that I assumed would lead to happily ever after. The problem was that Cody had plans for his life after graduation. Big plans. Plans that didn't include a life with Danny Hart's little sister.

I know now that it had been foolish to believe that I'd be able to talk Cody into discarding his plans to join the Navy and remain on the island with me. For one thing, he'd already enlisted, so despite my attempt to get him to stay, he already had an obligation to go.

In his defense, he did write to me when he got the opportunity. He apologized for our night of passion and assured me that it never should have happened. I was devastated. Beyond devastated; I was outraged that the man I loved would choose a life in the Navy over one with me.

"What's he doing here?" I asked.

"He says he'll be on the island for the summer. He asked about you. Wanted to know if you had a guy in your life."

"What did you tell him?" I felt myself begin to panic.

"I told him you were juggling a few guys but hadn't decided to make a commitment to any one suitor just yet."

I hugged Danny. He was one of the few people on the planet, along with Tara, who really got me.

"I wanted to swing by and warn you that he plans to look you up. I figured if I gave you a heads-up you'd be prepared for when you inevitably run into him."

"Thanks. I owe you."

"And that," Danny grinned, "is quite convenient because I just happen to need a favor."

I groaned. "What do you want?" Leave it to Danny to take a beautiful sibling moment and turn it into a negotiation.

"I have a date with Melanie Hannigan this weekend."

"So?" Melanie was a waitress at the pub who was *very* well endowed.

"So her cousin is in town and she wanted me to find him a date so we could double."

"You want me to go on a date with Melanie's cousin? What are you, my pimp?"

"It's just one date."

"Isn't there someone else you can ask to tag along? You know lots of girls," I pointed out.

"True, but you're the only girl I know who won't get jealous that I'm with

Melanie and she's stuck with Walter. So how about it?"

I glanced at Tara. I wanted to suggest that Danny take Tara instead, but that would be too cruel. "Okay, but just one date."

"Thanks, sis." Danny hugged me again.

Danny turned toward Tara, who had picked the kitten back up and was hugging him to her chest. "Did you do something different with your hair?" Danny asked my smitten friend.

"No. Why do you ask?"

Danny had the strangest look on his face as he stared at her. "No reason. Something just seems different about you." Danny turned back toward me. "Saturday at seven. I'll pick you up."

With that, he was out the door.

I turned back to Tara, who was smiling at the kitten. Yep, our little charmer had definitely found a home.

Chapter 6

Tuesday, May 19

I should have known it was going to be a very bad, horribly awful day as soon as I was awakened before first light by an angry banging on my front door. It seemed that I had forgotten to close the downstairs window, and apparently, Romeo had decided to take a midnight stroll to introduce himself to the fair maiden Juliet. I know: adorable, right? Unfortunately, Francine was a lot less charmed by the idea of a romance between her prized show cat and my temporary houseguest and wanted to be certain that I suffered the full extent of her wrath.

After listening to Francine rant for a good twenty minutes, I promised to make certain that Romeo would never come courting again and offered her a plate of the enchiladas Tara and I had made the previous evening. Francine is a ninety-eight-pound woman who's shorter than I am but can eat like a truck driver. Needless to say, she was temporarily pacified by my delicious offering and promised not to strangle my adorable visitor as long as he stayed on his side of the hedge.

By the time I was able to free myself from Francine's unwanted company I was fully awake, so I decided to get an early start on my day. That turned out to be the first in a series of really bad decisions. On the surface heading out to the beach for my run with Max a good two hours earlier than usual seemed like a harmless idea. The sun rises early during the spring and summer in this part of the country, so I still had a good two hours before I needed to meet Tara for our first class at the community center. A short run to stretch out and get Max some exercise couldn't possibly hurt. What I failed to take into account was that the long stretch of normally deserted sand that Max and I routinely enjoyed, is, at this time of day, infested with men and women lined up along the water's edge trying to catch their daily limit.

You know how, in the movies, they slow down the camera to show that pivotal moment when everything falls apart in extraslow motion? Well, I swear that's exactly what happened to me. One minute Max and I were jogging along, trying to ignore the buckets of fish lined up along the sand, and the next thing I knew, an extraexuberant fisherman was pulling on his line with a strong force to fling his fish from the water, up into the air, and onto the beach behind him.

I could see what was coming, but before I could yell at Max to stay, my playful companion veered from my side and dashed toward the bounty from the sea, which by this point was wildly flopping around on the sand.

"Hey, your dog stole my fish," a very large and very angry man yelled at me as Max trotted up with the fish in his mouth. The man didn't look familiar, so I had to assume he was a visitor from the mainland.

"I'm so sorry. I'm sure he didn't mean to. Drop it," I commanded my tail-wagging friend.

Max obediently lay the slightly mangled prize at my feet.

"I can't eat that now," the man complained.

"I really am very sorry. I don't know what happened. Max is normally very well behaved. Perhaps if you had controlled your catch a little better . . . I mean, you did fling it twenty feet behind you."

"Listen here, little lady—" The man grabbed my wrist a split second before Max clamped his jaw around his leg.

"Max, no!" I screamed.

He obediently let go of the man's leg and sat down beside me, but there was nothing I could do about the growling coming from deep within his throat.

"That dog is a menace and should be put down. I'm calling the sheriff."

"No, don't!" I pleaded. "Max didn't even break the skin on your leg. He was just warning you to back off. Any dog would have done the same. I'll pay for the fish," I offered.

The man took a step back. "You have any money on you?"

"No," I admitted, "but I live down the beach. I'll go get some and bring it right back."

The man seemed to be considering my offer. "Okay. A hundred bucks, and you got twenty minutes or I call the sheriff and report the fact that your dog attacked me."

"A hundred bucks?" I complained. "For that tiny fish?"

"Take it or leave it."

"Okay," I agreed. "I'll be right back."

Luckily, I kept a stash of emergency cash in my cabin, so I was able to avert a disaster by appeasing the unfriendly visitor to our island. I left Max at home with Romeo while I returned to give the man his money, which turned out to be my second really bad idea. Max was understandably riled up by the unpleasant encounter and was therefore determined not to let me out of his sight. Once I left, Max's protective instinct kicked in, resulting in a doggie-size hole in the screen door.

By the time Max caught up with me, I had delivered the money to the unreasonable fisherman and was on my way back to the house.

"What did you do?" I asked my dog. He suddenly realized the error of his ways and hung his head in shame. Max lay down at my feet with his face flat against the ground and looked up at me with the most apologetic eyes.

"I know. You were worried about me and wanted to protect me from the bad man. It's okay. I'm not mad." I smiled at my protector. "I guess we can call Danny to see if he has time to come by to fix this."

Max covered his eyes with his paw. I guess he knew that calling Danny before I jumped in the shower would be my third increasingly horrible decision of the day.

"Oh my gosh." Tara laughed. "You *are* kidding?"

"I'm afraid not." I groaned. I had just recounted my morning to Tara, including the fact that not only had Danny come right over while I was in the shower but that he had brought Cody with him. The problem was that I didn't know they were there and had come walking out of the bathroom in nothing but a very small towel.

"The towel was so small that when I turned to scamper back to my bedroom I'm pretty sure my right butt cheek was hanging out," I shared as we pulled up to the community center for our first exercise class.

"That is too funny. I wish I could have been there. What did the guys say?"

"Danny laughed and Cody whistled. I scurried away as soon as I noticed them, so I didn't really give them a chance to say anything. I snuck out my bedroom window and climbed down the tree when I left so I didn't have to face them."

"You didn't!"

"I had to. Trust me, that wasn't how I wanted my first encounter with Cody to go after everything that happened between us."

Tara and I paid for the class and continued into the room that was used for the various classes the center offered. Unfortunately, one entire wall was lined with mirrors, accentuating the fact that both Tara and I looked ridiculous in the leotards that had seemed like a good idea when we'd bought them the previous year for a dance class we'd never wound up attending. My bright green leotard clung to my slim frame, making me look like Peter Pan, and even worse, with her voluptuous figure, Tara looked like a grape about to pop in the purple leotard she'd chosen to wear.

"Maybe we should put our sweats back on," I suggested.

Tara frowned at her refection in the mirror. "Yeah, it is a little chilly in here."

Although the temperature in the room actually resembled that of a sauna, Tara and I remained fully clothed for the entire hour. The class was fairly intense for a beginners' group, but as far as I was concerned it was still fun. Poor Tara, though, looked like she was going to die by the time our instructor called for us to begin our cooldown. I hoped Tara would stick with the class this time around. I'd tried to get her to commit to a regular exercise routine in the past, but every time we registered for a class Tara would end up with an excuse to quit before we even began.

"Wonderful job," our instructor, Bitzy Biner, who looked like an airbrushed Barbie doll, complimented us as the class began to break up. "I hope you both enjoyed yourselves and plan to return."

"I had a good time," I said, though I was pretty sure Tara was too winded to speak. "I think Tara and I can fit two mornings a week into our schedules."

My friend didn't say anything, but I was willing to bet that if she could, she'd offer a counter to my statement.

"I heard you were the one who found Keith Weaver's body," Bitzy added.

"Yes. Unfortunately, I stumbled over him while Tara and I were taking a look at the cannery. It's such a shame."

"Oh, I don't know about that." Bitzy shrugged. "Most of the folks who showed up at the meeting last night seemed to think that Keith's death wasn't the worst thing that could happen."

"Meeting?" I asked.

"The show-and-tell seminar about the condo development Bill Powell is proposing," Bitzy explained. "Most everyone seemed to think Keith Weaver was intent on blocking the project before it ever got off the ground. Personally, I'd like to see some affordable housing on the island."

I frowned. "I thought the scuttlebutt was that Keith had changed his mind and decided to support the project. I heard he planned to help push it through the island council."

"That's not what people were saying last night. Bill Powell wanted us all to think the project was a slam dunk so those of us who were interested in buying the units would put down deposits, but behind the scenes the chatter was contradictory at best. More than one person there told me that Keith had made a move to stop last night's meeting from even happening. It seems he was in possession of some pretty compelling evidence that the island's current infrastructure would never hold up with all the new units. The general feeling in the room seemed to suggest that if Keith hadn't died, the entire project would have been dead in the water."

"Bill Powell was trying to get people to put money down on the units even though the project hasn't been approved yet?"

"Yup. And there were people lining up with their checkbooks out. Bill is offering some sort of a discount to anyone who commits in the next few days. I don't have all the details, but I suppose if you're interested you could ask that handsome district manager from the bank."

"Mr. Bradford was at the meeting?" I asked.

"Yeah, he was there representing the bank. I guess they're backing the project, so he was there to talk to people about financing."

I frowned. I suppose it made sense that the bank would provide the funding, but something felt off about the whole thing.

Bitzy wandered away to speak to other class members, and Tara and I made our way out to my car. "Didn't you say Kim told you that Keith had decided to back Bill's project?" I asked her as she slid into the passenger seat.

"That's what Kim told me, but I guess she was wrong."

"I feel like something isn't adding up. We need to speak to Kim again. If Keith was against the project we have an entirely different set of suspects than if he supported it."

Tara pulled her sweatband off and tossed it in her gym bag. "Why do you even care who the suspects are?"

"Because if we don't have suspects we won't be able to figure out who killed Keith Weaver."

Tara turned to look at me. "And why on earth would you think it was up to us to figure out who killed Keith Weaver?"

I turned the key and prayed my old clunker of a car would start. "We found his body," I pointed out. "That's like a sign from the universe that we're supposed to be involved."

Tara rolled down her window. "I have to say your logic is . . . well, illogical."

"No it's not," I argued. "It's like that thing where if you save someone's life you're responsible for them. Likewise, if you find a dead body you're responsible for finding out how the person died."

"You're insane. You know that, right?"

"Come on, Tara. What do we have to lose by snooping around a bit?"

"Our lives, for a start. Besides, Finn won't want us to get involved. He's perfectly capable of figuring this out without our help."

"He doesn't have to know we're snooping," I argued.

Tara let out a long breath. "I know you're a huge mystery buff and the chance to investigate a local murder must be tempting, but I want to point out that, unlike most of the heroines in the books you read, we're neither strong nor brave. We don't have superpowers and neither of us is an extraordinary physical specimen. I shop in the plus size department and you shop in the children's department. Trust me when I say that I really don't think the universe is depending on us to save the day."

I put my car into gear and pulled out into traffic. "Yeah, maybe you're right."

"Come on, cheer up," Tara tried. "I'll take you to breakfast."

"Actually, I told Mr. Parsons and Mrs. Trexler I'd stop by this morning to drop off the enchiladas we made last night."

"That's probably just as well. I really want to finish up the new proposal for Mr. Bradford. I'm hoping if we can get it approved we can begin the remodel as soon as the building is released by the crime scene unit. I'll call you later."

Chapter 7

After I dropped Tara at her house I went back to my cabin and took another shower. Luckily, it appeared that both Max and Romeo had behaved themselves while I was gone, so maybe my string of bad luck was at an end. I pulled my unruly hair into a knot, slipped into my most comfortable pair of jeans and a sweatshirt, and headed into the kitchen to pack up my offering for my reclusive friends.

Mr. Parsons's property was to the left of my aunt's. He lived alone in the house, as he had ever since I was old enough to remember. I'm not sure why he never married or had children, but most of the time he seemed content to hang out alone in the huge old house his grandfather had built. I brought him food a couple of times a week and he'd listen politely as I rambled on about whatever it was that was happening in my life.

Although Mr. Parsons had no pets, he seemed to like Max, so I made a point of bringing him along on most of my visits.

"Mr. Parsons, it's Cait and Max," I called after I'd both buzzed the intercom and knocked on the door.

"You can come in," Mr. Parsons answered. "I'm in the study."

I could hear the lock give as he remotely opened the front door. The house Mr. Parsons lived in was large and drafty. I have no idea why his grandfather had built such a monstrosity. As far as I knew, the man had only had two children, but the cavernous house must have at least ten bedrooms.

Mr. Parsons lived on the bottom floor, and I was fairly certain he rarely ventured to the second or third story of the house. The bottom level featured a large living room that, based on the dust layered on the furniture, was rarely used; a study that was really a warm and cozy library; a ballroom that had never hosted a ball in my lifetime; a kitchen, several bathrooms, and a single bedroom behind the kitchen that had most likely been designed to accommodate the hired help.

Mr. Parsons had made a home within a home by utilizing the downstairs bedroom, the nearby bath, the kitchen, and the study.

"I brought you some enchiladas," I greeted the man, who smiled when Max trotted over to say hi. "Would you like me to heat some up for you now?"

"No. Just leave them in the refrigerator. I'll have them later."

I left Max with Mr. Parsons while I headed to the kitchen to do as he'd asked. The room really could use a good cleaning. Maybe I'd come back to straighten up before I left. I opened the refrigerator and frowned. The shelves that should have contained food were almost barren. I closed the door and returned to the study.

"I was wondering if you could do me a favor," I said.

"Depends."

"I really need to run to the grocery store to pick up a few things. Do you mind if I leave Max here with you?"

"I guess that would be okay."

"I noticed you were out of eggs. I'll get some for you while I'm there. Is there anything else I can pick up?"

Mr. Parsons hesitated.

"I really don't mind, and you're taking care of Max for me," I encouraged.

"Guess I could use some bread, and maybe a nice piece of fish for my dinner."

"Okay. I'll see what I can find. And thanks for watching Max. I won't be but a few minutes."

"Take your time. Max and I will be fine."

I paused. "If you really don't mind keeping an eye on Max I do have a couple of other errands I could see to."

"Like I said, take your time. Max and I are going to see what's on television this morning."

"Then I'll see you in a couple of hours."

I decided to stop in at Mrs. Trexler's before heading to the store, where I planned to buy enough groceries to fill up Mr. Parsons's refrigerator and pantry. I knew he would enjoy spending some time with Max, and Max always enjoyed spending time with Mr. Parsons. I'd unsuccessfully tried to talk him into adopting one of our cats, but maybe a dog? I'm not the sort to try to second guess everyone's motive for doing what they do—okay, maybe I am—but I did think Mr. Parsons's lifestyle could only be enhanced by the addition of a pet.

After I dropped off Mrs. Trexler's enchiladas and sat down to visit for a while, I decided to stop by the Bait and Stitch, the shop my aunt owns with her best friend Marley, to ask about the lab mix Marley's neighbor was trying to find a home for. The Bait and Stitch is located in the tourist town of Pelican Bay, and while the eclectic little shop has a local following, its location near the wharf, where the ferry docks, brings in a good amount of tourist traffic as well.

"Mornin'," I greeted the occupants of the brightly lit shop, which included Marley and five other women sitting at a large, round table working on the quilt I knew they intended to donate to the church bazaar.

"Mornin', Cait," the group answered back.

"Where's Aunt Maggie?" I asked. Normally, you would find her working the counter at this time of day.

"She wasn't feeling well, so she decided to stay home," Marley informed me.

"I didn't realize she was worse today," I said. "Francine stopped by early this morning to read me the riot act after Romeo decided to sneak under the hedge and romance Juliet, and somehow the day got away from me. I'd better stop in to check on her."

"I would feel better if you did," Marley told me. "I have to say, I'm really getting worried about her. Every time I think she's getting better she has a setback."

I frowned. "I know what you mean. She seems to have settled into this pattern where she'll become really ill, miss a week or two of work, start to feel better, resume her normal routine, and then get sick again. I think she overdoes things when she starts to get better and then has a relapse."

"I agree." Marley looked worried. "I've tried to talk to her about taking things slowly, but you know Maggie."

"I talked to Siobhan, who promised to talk to her. I'm hoping Maggie will go to Seattle for some additional testing."

"If there's anything I can do to help with your campaign just let me know," Marley offered. "By the way, did you get the message I left for you about that out-of-town whale watching group?"

"No. I've been running around all morning and haven't stopped to check my messages."

"A group of men came in early to buy some bait and we got to talking. They were asking about a whale watching tour for this evening. I called Danny, but he didn't answer, so I left a message, and I left one on your cell as well. They're fishing this morning, but I told them to check back this afternoon."

The whale watching tour boat Danny runs maintains a regular schedule during the summer, but during the off-season the charters are run on a reservations-only basis. Right now the reservations are taken via cell phone and referral, but once

Tara and I open Coffee Cat Books, we plan to provide a permanent reservation desk near the coffee bar.

"I'll stop by Danny's boat to see if I can track him down," I promised. "The main reason I stopped by was to ask you about that lab mix your neighbor is trying to find a new home for. Is he still available?"

"You looking to get another dog?"

"No. But I have a friend who might be interested."

"As far as I know the little guy hasn't found a home yet," Marley said.

Marley had already told me that the dog's owners had recently gotten divorced and the wife wanted nothing to do with the dog, while the husband had plans to sign on with a fishing boat for the summer.

"Do you think they'd let me take him for a trial?" I asked.

"I don't see why not. Hang on and I'll see if I can get him on the line."

I chatted with the women's quilting circle while I waited for Marley to make her call. The Bait and Stitch was not only a unique shop with a welcoming feel but a gathering spot for the locals as well. The quilting circle met several times a week, and most days at the beginning and end of the day local fishermen gathered to drink the free coffee and shoot the breeze as well. In addition, both the Mystery Lovers Book Club, of which I was a member, and the Romance Readers Book Club, which Marley attends, met at the shop after-hours. Tara and I had already spoken to both clubs about relocating their gatherings to Coffee Cat Books once we got up and running.

"My neighbor is fine with you taking Rambler for a trial," Marley came back to tell me. "You can pick him up right now if you want."

"I need to run by the store, but I'll stop by to get him after that."

I said my good-byes and was headed out the door when Patience Tillman, one of the women who was part of the senior women's group at the church walked in.

"Mornin'," I said.

"Caitlin, how are you?"

"Fine, and you?"

"Worried, actually."

"Worried?" I asked as all eyes in the store settled on us.

"Francine was supposed to do a presentation at the women's group this morning but never showed up. I called her phone and she didn't answer, so I stopped by her house and there was no answer there either."

"Maybe she had a last-minute emergency and had to go out," I suggested. "I just saw her this morning and she seemed fine. Maybe she forgot about the meeting and went somewhere with a friend."

The woman frowned. "I just spoke to her yesterday and she was very excited about having the opportunity to have the women's group back her as a candidate for the island council. Our group wields quite a bit of influence, as you know."

"Yes, I know." It occurred to me that these women, who regularly met at the Bait and Stitch for free, ought to be backing Maggie, but I didn't say as much.

"When you spoke with her yesterday did she indicate that she wasn't feeling well or that something was wrong?" I asked.

"No, she seemed perfectly fine."

"Then I wouldn't worry. If I run into her I'll have her call you," I assured the woman.

"Thank you. I'd appreciate it."

I left the Bait and Stitch and headed to the marina to see if I could track Danny down. That, I would soon find out, turned out to be my fourth really bad idea of the day.

The marina, where Danny keeps his boat, was located in the harbor where the old cannery Tara and I hoped to turn into Coffee Cat Books was located. I parked my car and started down the boardwalk toward the water, noticing as I went that there were several men walking around inside the building. There are misinformed people who will tell you that my impulsive nature coupled with my natural curiosity can be a lethal combination. While I'll admit that my tendency to act first and think later has gotten me into some less than ideal situations, I've also found that acting on my thoughts can occasionally be a perspicacious thing to do. This, unfortunately, wasn't one of those times.

A quick glance told me that Camden Bradford was with the men who had gathered inside, to investigate the crime scene, I imagined. To be honest, I'm not sure why he was included in the fact-gathering group, but perhaps the fact that the bank he worked for owned the property played into the equation. I found that my urge to listen in on the conversation the men seemed to be embroiled in was more than I could control. Upon further investigation, it didn't appear that the men were from the sheriff's office, as I had first assumed.

Could these men actually be responsible for Keith Weaver's death? The more I thought about it, the more I realized that Mr. Bradford made an excellent suspect.

Bitzy had said that Keith Weaver was trying to block the condo development, which Mr. Bradford's bank was backing financially. Kim had indicated to Tara that Weaver had expressed his intention to not only support the project but to push it through at the council level. What if Weaver had agreed to work with Powell and then changed his mind?

Keith Weaver was found dead in a building Mr. Bradford had access to. I knew it was a bit of a reach, but I suddenly felt fairly certain that Mr. Bradford had lured Keith to the cannery, where he'd then hit him over the head. The thing I couldn't figure out was why he'd killed him in a building to which he was connected.

I realized that the answer to this question could very well be the topic of conversation among the men who suddenly looked more like gangsters than law enforcement personnel. If Tara were here she'd say that my perception of the men had changed to accommodate my theory, and perhaps she'd be right, but there was no way I was going to find out for certain if I couldn't get closer to the group so I could listen in.

The men were standing at the back of the building, near the water side of the structure. I couldn't very well walk through the front door, but I certainly could sneak around behind it. I noticed that one of the windows was cracked open just a bit, so if I could get close enough I was certain I'd be able to hear what they were saying. The problem was, the only thing on the water side of the building was . . . water.

I took a moment to consider my options. The old cannery had been built atop the wharf, which was actually quite a bit above the waterline. There were beams between the decking of the wharf and the water. It wouldn't be unreasonable to think that I could use the beams to make my way across the water and access the small ledge on the exterior of the building. Making the decision that my plan would work, I climbed onto the first beam. The thing I really hadn't thought through was that sea lions tended to nap on the beams during high tide, making for a very slippery surface. (Yep, the beams were covered in sea lion poop.) Somehow I managed to make my way to the far side of the structure and was planning to climb up onto the ledge when a playful sea lion came up out of the water and nipped me in the butt.

"Stop that," I admonished.

The sea lion barked at me but didn't swim away as I'd hoped he would.

"I suppose I'm in your napping spot?"

The fact that the sea lion dove down didn't comfort me because I could almost predict what would happen next. I quickly grabbed for the ledge, which was just beyond my reach when the sea lion resurfaced and shoved me off my perch.

After swimming to the shore and pulling myself out of the water, I called Danny and left another message about the whale watching tour and then went home and took my third shower of the day. I changed my clothes and pulled my hair back into a braid, then headed to the grocery store, where I bought a week's worth of groceries for Mr. Parsons, as well as dog food, a dog bed, a dog bowl, and several dog toys. I loaded everything into my car and drove over to pick up the dog and then back to Mr. Parsons's, where I hoped to find him open to my offer of a job.

I'd left the kitchen door unlocked, so I put away the groceries before I went in search of my neighbor and my dog. I found them curled up on the sofa watching a movie together. Of course the minute I walked in with Rambler, Max jumped off the sofa to come over to greet his canine friend.

"Who do we have here?" Mr. Parsons asked.

"This is Rambler," I answered. Thankfully, Rambler was a quiet and well-mannered dog who walked politely across the room to greet the elderly man.

"I actually brought him by to meet you because I'm in a bit of a tough spot and could really use some help."

"What kind of help?" Mr. Parsons asked.

"A friend of Marley's asked me to watch his dog for the summer while he's fishing in Alaska," I offered as a half truth. "I told him I'd do it, but now with Maggie being sick, I just don't know if I can handle the extra responsibility."

Rambler placed his paw in Mr. Parsons's lap. Mr. Parsons smiled and began petting him behind the ears. I took that as a good sign.

"I don't suppose you'd be interested in helping me out."

Mr. Parsons paused. I hoped he was considering my request.

"And all I'd have to do is let him stay here with me?"

"Yep, that's it. You have plenty of room and a large yard. Rambler is well behaved. I don't think he'll be a problem."

"I guess I could do that. For you." Rambler put his head in the man's lap. "You're always so thoughtful, bringing me your leftovers. I guess it's the least I can do."

"Excellent." I sighed in relief. "The owner sent along some food and supplies. They're in the kitchen; I put them away when I first got back. You have my number, so call me if you need anything. I'll be back to visit on Friday, like I always do."

"I'm sure we'll be fine. You and Max can hurry along now." Rambler had crawled onto the sofa and was lying next to his new dad. "I'll see you both on Friday."

I smiled as Max and I made our way back to my car. There's no better feeling than putting two souls who need one another in touch for the first time.

Chapter 8

Later that evening I began closing windows in preparation for bed. I'd had a long day and I was exhausted. Between my early morning wakeup call, my run-in with the fisherman, my unfortunate swim in the ocean, and my afternoon arguing with Maggie about going to Seattle for medical testing, I found that I was ready to put the stress of the day behind me. Max had been following me around the cabin as I worked, but so far I'd seen no sign of Romeo.

"Oh Romeo, sweet Romeo. 'Wherefore art thou Romeo?'" I called.

No answer.

I tried again. "It's time for bed. You like the fuzzy blanket under the comforter," I reminded him.

I looked at Max. "Do you know where our little Casanova went off to?"

Max tilted his head as if he was considering the question but seemed as stumped as I was. Romeo had been in the cabin earlier. I'd fed him and he'd sat on my lap while we watched a movie on television. When the movie was over I'd gone out to take care of the cats in the sanctuary. I'd left Max and Romeo in the cabin, but now that I thought about it, I hadn't seen Romeo since I'd come back in. I didn't think I'd left the door open, but the window had been cracked a few inches to let the warm spring air inside. Could Romeo have squeezed through? Danny had taken the screen for the window with him when he was here this morning. It had been torn for months and he'd decided that as long as he was going to fix the screen door he might as well fix the screen on the window as well.

"Juliet," I realized.

I looked at Max. "You stay here and keep an eye out for our little tomcat. I'm going to go check next door. If Francine realizes that Romeo has come courting so soon after her lecture she's going to kill both of us. If I'm not back in twenty minutes call 911."

Max barked as if he understood, but even I didn't believe he really could call for help should I run into a wrathful Francine.

Luckily, it was low tide, which allowed me to sneak around the hedge that separated the two properties without getting wet. I was actually hoping Francine would still be away, as she had been for most of the day. Things would go easier if she never found out that Romeo was trespassing again. Unfortunately, when I rounded the corner to her house the light in her living area was on. I didn't want to call out for Romeo in case she heard me, so I silently slunk toward the back of Francine's house. I doubted she would let Juliet get out twice in one day, so chances were that Romeo was near the back of the house, looking in.

I crawled onto the back deck and looked in through the large picture window. I almost let out a screech when I saw none other than Camden Bradford standing in the middle of Francine's living room.

What in the heck was Mr. Bradford doing in Francine's living room?

I squatted down so that only the top of my head could be seen through the window. I hoped the man wouldn't turn around; the last thing I needed was another embarrassing encounter to add to my Camden Bradford Embarrassing Encounter portfolio. I looked around the room but didn't see Francine or Juliet. It appeared Mr. Bradford was on the phone. I crawled along the ground toward an open window in the hope of overhearing his conversation.

"It's all taken care of," I heard him say. "It was really no problem at all. I'm glad to help with the cleanup. It's the least I can do."

Cleanup? Was the man here to clean Francine's house? And then I noticed that the furniture was all shoved to the side of the room and the area rug that was normally under the furniture had been rolled up and placed near the door leading down to the basement.

"Don't worry; I'll take care of her," Mr. Bradford said.

Take care of her? Take care of who?

"No one will ever know; now I gotta go."

Mr. Bradford glanced in my direction. I slumped down so as not to be seen. When I didn't hear anything more going on I looked back through the window after a moment. The door to the basement was open and the rolled-up rug was gone.

Francine?

I watched through the window as Mr. Bradford came back upstairs. He looked around the room and then headed toward the kitchen. I was trying to decide whether to try to sneak in and check out the basement when I saw the exterior light at the back of the house come on. I managed to leap off the two-foot-high deck and into the thick shrubbery a split second before Bradford opened the back door. He stood there looking around before closing the door and returning inside.

I scurried across the yard and then back around the hedge to my own side while trying to figure out what to do. Should I call Finn? It seemed like the logical choice, given the fact that I was certain Francine Rivers was wrapped up in her living room carpet.

Then the question became, why kill Francine? She was a candidate for the island council, as well as an outspoken opponent of the condo development. Bradford had said he would 'take care of her.' Could Francine be the *her* he was referring to, or was there yet another target in Camden Bradford's evil plan?

With Keith out of the way, the council vote on the project would be tied. Whoever took Keith's place would represent the deciding vote. I figured the person chosen to replace Keith would most likely come from the pool of candidates running for the open position. Like Francine, Maggie was an opponent of the project. The other two candidates, Drake Moore and Porter Wilson, had been vocal in their support of it.

When I got back to my cabin I was greeted by Romeo, who was sitting on the swing on my front deck.

"Where have you been, you naughty cat?"

Romeo began to purr. I tried to be mad but had to smile. I picked him up and then went inside, where I promptly called Finn. When Finn answered I explained what I had seen and what I suspected.

"Camden Bradford is a well-respected businessman who would have no reason to kill either Keith or Francine," Finn insisted.

"Maybe his motive has something to do with the fact that his bank is backing the condo project," I suggested.

"It seems unlikely. The bank backs all sorts of business ventures. I doubt Camden Bradford gets emotionally involved with his projects."

"So where's Francine and why was Mr. Bradford at her house?" I asked.

Finn sighed. "I don't know. If I stop by to see what I can find out will you go to bed and let me handle it?"

"Yeah, okay," I agreed. "And Finn . . ."

"Yeah?"

"Be careful."

Chapter 9

Wednesday, May 20

The next morning I got up early and made Aunt Maggie a big breakfast in the hope of enticing her to eat. The past few days her appetite had been all but nonexistent. Maggie was known for her sweet tooth, so I decided on homemade waffles with fresh boysenberries.

"You're up early," Maggie commented as she came downstairs dressed for work.

"I wanted to make you breakfast."

"I appreciate that, dear, but I'm really not hungry."

"I made waffles." I took the cover off the stack on the warmer. "With boysenberries and powdered sugar," I bribed.

Maggie hesitated. "They do look good. Maybe I'll try a half."

I spooned berries over the freshly grilled waffle and sprinkled it with the sugar, then I set it on the table, along with a big glass of milk.

"I think I'd like a cup of tea," Maggie requested.

I put the water on to boil. Personally, I'm much more of a coffee drinker, but Maggie seems to love her tea, which in my opinion is so bitter as to be unpalatable.

"I've already seen to the cats," I informed my aunt as I poured the hot water over the tea leaves. "I think the large ragdoll we took in over the winter is ready for a home. I thought I'd ask around. If I don't find a home for him here I'll take him to the next auction."

"He's a beautiful cat," Maggie said as she served herself another half waffle. "I'm sure we won't have a problem finding him a home. So what are your plans for the day?"

"I'm going to stop by Francine's, and then I need to sit down with Danny to go over the reservations for the next few days. I'm having lunch with Tara so we can finalize the reworked proposal for the bank. And I thought I'd stop in at the Bait and Stitch after that. I'd be happy to help Marley, if you want to make it an early day."

I poured myself a second cup of coffee and was about to serve Maggie the tea that had been steeping when Romeo jumped up onto the counter and knocked Maggie's tea to the floor.

"Romeo," I yelled as one of Maggie's favorite cups shattered. "What has gotten into you?"

Romeo meowed and looked at me as I hurriedly picked up the pieces of broken china before any of the animals stepped on them.

"That's okay." Maggie picked up Romeo, who had wandered over to her in a gesture that looked a lot like an apology. "Accidents happen."

"I'll make you another cup after I get this cleaned up," I offered.

"No, I think I'll skip it this morning. I wanted to talk to you before you headed out for the day."

"Oh, okay. What about?" I asked as I got the mop out of the broom closet and began to soak up the rest of the tea from the floor.

"I spent a good part of the night thinking about our discussion yesterday," Maggie began.

"I'm sorry we argued," I offered as I returned the mop to the closet and sat down across from her. "You know I love you, but I worry that you aren't getting any better."

"I know." Maggie placed her hand over mine. "I've decided to go for additional testing. I'm going to the mainland on the one o'clock ferry. I'll probably stay through the weekend, but I should be home sometime on Monday. I hoped you could help Marley at the store while I was gone."

"I'd be happy to." I smiled. "And thank you for doing this."

"What's this about visiting with Francine?" Maggie asked.

I took a huge bite of the waffle I'd served myself to delay answering. On one hand, I really wanted Maggie's input on the situation. On the other, if she knew that something might have happened to Francine she would most likely cancel her trip.

"I wanted to ask her about Keith Weaver," I compromised. "I've been thinking about his murder, and it seems to me that the motive could very well have to do with Bill Powell's condo project."

"How so?" Maggie asked.

"It occurred to me that Keith's vote regarding the project could be pivotal. As of the last meeting, there were three members, including Keith, who were against and two members who supported the project. Tara told me recently she'd heard from Kim that Keith had switched sides and was planning to vote to approve the project. If that's really true it seems to me that someone who's strongly against the project might want Keith out of the way."

"Wouldn't it be a bit extreme to kill someone over a difference of opinion?"

"I think we're talking about more than just an opinion here. The project has raised some really serious emotions. Those who want to see the lifestyle on the island preserved feel very strongly that the project, and others like it, should be blocked, while those who are barely scrapping by are counting on the project to bring new revenue to the island."

Maggie took a sip of her milk. "You do have a point. I have to admit I haven't kept up with things the way I used to since I've been ill, but I hadn't heard anything about Keith switching sides."

"That's the thing; I'm not a hundred percent certain he had. Kim worked with him. She saw him every day, so you'd think she would know where he stood on the issue, but Bitzy, who's interested in buying one of the new units and supports the project, told Tara and me that Keith seemed to be intent on blocking the project. I'm not sure what's going on, but I do know that something doesn't add up."

"What does this have to do with Francine?" Maggie asked suspiciously.

"I figure that with Keith gone, his spot on the board will be filled by one of the four candidates running for the open seat. I think the assignment of Keith's seat is going to be hotly contested because it will represent the deciding vote. You and Francine oppose the project while Drake Moore and Porter Wilson support it."

Maggie frowned. I realized a moment too late that I might have said too much. I could see the wheels in her mind turning and was certain she was on the verge of canceling her trip.

"I'm sure the council won't do anything about replacing Keith until next month's meeting," I added. "Hopefully, by then the specialist you're going to see will have identified the problem and you'll be back to your old self."

"Maybe I should have a chat with Francine myself before I go," Maggie said.

"It's already getting late and you wanted to stop by the Bait and Stitch before you left," I reminded her. "Why don't you go ahead and do what you were going to do and I'll let Francine know you want to get together next week?"

Maggie hesitated.

"It would be to your advantage to be at your best when you talk," I reminded her.

"I suppose you're right. You'll call me if you learn anything new?"

"I will. And you'll only be gone for a few days. I doubt anything at all will happen in such a short amount of time."

Boy, was I wrong.

I finished eating breakfast and then saw Maggie off on her errands and did the dishes. When I'd checked with Finn earlier he'd reported that he'd been by Francine's, as he'd promised the previous evening, but the house had been dark and no one had answered when he knocked. I'd asked why he didn't just break in and check out the basement, but he'd explained that he didn't have probable cause to do so. I was certain by this point that Camden Bradford was guilty of killing Francine, and probably Keith as well, but I needed some sort of proof before I would be able to get anyone to take me seriously.

"I'm certain Mr. Bradford has nothing to do with Keith's murder," Tara said as we shared lunch while we worked on the proposal for Coffee Cat Books.

"What about Francine?" I asked.

"You don't even know she's dead."

"I saw Camden Bradford in her house. When Finn went by later the house was dark. I went by this morning and there was no answer. I'm telling you, Francine is rolled up in her area rug, which I assume is still in her basement."

Tara sat back and looked directly at me. "You need to get off this whole conspiracy thing. The only way we're going to follow our dream of opening Coffee Cat Books is if we can get the full amount of funding we need from the bank. We're *never* going to get our loan approved if you're running around town accusing the man who has the power to support our loan of murder. Please tell me that you'll drop this."

There was no way I was going to drop it. Tara should know me well enough to realize that. On the other hand, I really didn't want to engage in a debate that had no acceptable resolution.

"Promise me," Tara insisted.

"I promise I won't run around town accusing Bradford of murder."

"Good." Tara sighed in relief. "So about the windows . . ." She launched into the subject we were supposed to be discussing in the first place.

I'd promised I wouldn't run around town accusing the district manager of the bank of murder and I didn't. In fact, I didn't run anywhere. I finished my conversation with Tara and then headed over to the Bait and Stitch to help Marley, as I'd promised Maggie I would. I might have casually brought up the subject of Keith Weaver's death to a few of the patrons who stopped by that afternoon. Of course, my sneaky interrogation of the Bait and Stitch customers yielded me nothing more than I could have gained from sitting at the bar at O'Malley's and listening to casual conversation.

"I heard Cody West is back," one of the women from the quilting circle commented.

"I heard that as well," Marley answered. "He's such a handsome young man, with those dark blue eyes and all that thick brown hair. I stopped off to pick up some coffee on my way in and overheard the gals from the Clip and Curl arguing over which of them had the right to take him out for a spin."

"Out for a spin?" I asked as I rolled my eyes.

"I think that was their way of referring to dating," Marley informed me.

"I know what it means to take someone out for a spin; it just seems archaic to compare him to an object that can be had by the winning bidder."

"Oh, I don't think they were actually bidding on him, dear. I think they were deciding among themselves who would have the right to pursue him."

It's hard to have a proper rant when the person you're ranting to takes everything you say so literally. Of course, I'm not sure why I cared if the women at the Clip and Curl were arm wrestling over Cody. They could have him, because lord knew I certainly didn't want anything to do with him.

"I'm afraid the girls might be wasting their time fighting over Cody," one of the other women sitting at the quilting table chimed in. "I saw Cody at church on Sunday and he was sitting next to Samantha Waller. They seemed to be pretty chummy."

Samantha Waller was the homecoming queen the year Cody was homecoming king. They'd dated for a while in high school, although they'd parted ways by the time Cody and I hooked up. Samantha had married a local boy right after graduating, but they'd since divorced. I guess it made sense that now that they were both living on the same island and single at least for the time being, they might renew their relationship. I'm not sure why that angered me, but it did.

"Samantha needs to settle down with someone like Cody," someone said. "She married that loser who got her pregnant and now she's on her own with twin boys to raise. Cody was always such a responsible sort. The type to honor his commitments. Samantha could certainly do worse."

"I heard Cody is volunteering at the church this summer. He's going to put his muscle to use and finally get the building painted."

"It's about time," one of the women grumbled.

There were two churches on the island: St. Patrick's Catholic Church and Madrona Island Community Church. The Catholic Church was in desperate need of a facelift, so I assumed that was the one the women were referring to.

"I know Velmalee is thrilled to have Cody back on the island," Marley informed the group. Velmalee Arlington ran the community theater group, and even though Cody was most known for his contribution to the Madrona High School football team, he'd starred in his share of musicals as well. "I'm assuming he'll rejoin the church choir as well."

"Can we stop talking about St. Cody and get back to the subject of Keith Weaver's death?" I suggested.

"I thought we'd exhausted that subject," Marley said.

"The subject can't be exhausted until the killer is caught," I argued, not because I was that concerned about finding the killer but because I was over listening to everyone rave about the island's favorite son.

After Marley and I closed for the day I said my good-byes and headed home. I knew that both Max and Romeo would be waiting for me and I had the cats in the sanctuary to tend to, but I decided to take a few extra minutes to stop off at Francine's one more time. I parked at my cabin and headed next door via the beach. I knocked on the door and waited, but there was no answer. I walked back around the house and looked in through the tiny basement window. It was dark, and I couldn't really see anything, so I did what any logical person would do—I broke the window and squeezed inside. The minute my feet landed on the cement floor I heard a car pull up in the drive. I hoped whoever it was would realize Francine wasn't home and quickly be on their way.

I stood still for a moment and listened. I didn't hear anyone walking around overhead. Perhaps the car had left. It was dark in the sublevel room, so I used the flashlight on my phone to have a better look around. The basement was large and stuffed with old furniture and discarded boxes. It was going to take a while to find the rug. I carefully made my way through the room so I wouldn't make a lot of noise in case whoever had arrived in the car I'd heard hadn't left as I'd hoped. All I had to do was find Francine's body, forward a photo of it to Finn, and then sit back and let him deal with the rest.

"What are you doing in here?"

I turned around to find Camden Bradford standing in the doorway with a bat in his hand.

"Don't kill me," I blurted out.

"Why would I kill you?" He lowered the bat.

"You're holding a bat," I pointed out.

"I heard a noise and thought it might be a prowler, which I guess it was. What are you doing in here?"

"Looking for proof."

"Proof of what?"

"Proof that you killed Francine."

"What?" He looked both shocked and confused.

"You heard me." I tried to appear both taller and braver than anyone was ever going to believe.

"Why do you think I killed Francine?" Mr. Bradford asked.

I explained about looking for Romeo and what I'd seen the previous night.

"You think Francine is wrapped up in that rug?" He glanced toward the rug.

"Isn't she?"

"Of course not."

Mr. Bradford walked across the room and unrolled the rug. It was empty.

"Then where's Francine and why are you at her house?"

"Francine is a good friend of my mother's. My mom is having some personal issues. I've tried to help her out, but quite frankly, she's making me nuts. I asked Francine if she would be willing to go visit her to see if she could help her through this difficult time. She was happy to do so, but she's planning a Founders Day party and had already scheduled a cleaning crew to come in and take care of some things, like cleaning the floors."

"So you volunteered to move the rug."

"Exactly."

"I heard you say you would take care of her. What was that about?"

"Juliet. I'm supposed to take care of Juliet."

"Oh." Unfortunately, it all made sense. "So where's Juliet?"

"Francine dropped her off at a friend's because she had to leave in such a hurry. I went to pick her up this morning and brought her back here. I'm going to stay here at the house until Francine gets back."

"Oh."

"Why would you think I killed Francine in the first place?"

"Because it made sense after I figured out it was you who killed Keith Weaver."

I have to admit the man didn't even blink. Maybe he was getting used to my random thoughts and behavior. "I didn't kill Keith Weaver."

"His body was found in your building," I pointed out. "The lock wasn't damaged. Whoever killed him either has a key to the building or the code to the lockbox. In my book, that narrows the suspects down to you."

"Keith had a key to the building because he was handling the sale," Bradford explained. "He might even have been showing the building to a prospective buyer when he was killed."

"But if you didn't kill him who did?"

"That's a question I've been asking myself since his body was found."

Chapter 10

Thursday, May 21

"So let me get this straight," Tara said the next morning as we sat on the deck in front of my cabin, having coffee after our exercise class. "You broke a window and snuck into Francine's house in order to prove that Mr. Bradford was guilty of murder?"

"Sounds about right." I poured cream into my coffee as Romeo napped in the swing and Max trotted around the yard, where several of the cats from the sanctuary lounged on the lawn.

"You promised me you'd leave this alone," Tara reminded me. "We could have lost our only chance at a loan. We could have lost our dream."

"But we didn't. Cam wasn't even mad that I'd broken in, or that I'd accused him of murder."

Tara picked up the kitten she'd had her eye on when it wandered over. Tara's the type who likes to think things through rather than making rash decisions, but the kitten and I already knew she'd be taking him home any day now.

"Cam?"

"He told me to call him Cam," I informed Tara. "I told him he could call me Ms. Hart."

"You didn't."

I shrugged. "It was a joke. He knew it. It's all good."

"So you are off the idea that Camden Bradford is the killer?"

"Not at all," I answered as I watched one of the pair of bald eagles that had been hanging out in the area land on a rock exposed by the low tide. "I said the guy was nice; I didn't say he was innocent."

"But you said he explained everything," Tara pointed out.

"He explained Francine's absence and his presence in her house. That doesn't mean he didn't kill Keith."

"If you do anything to mess up our loan . . ." Tara warned.

"Don't worry," I said with more confidence than I felt. "It's in the bag."

"I hope so." Tara nuzzled the kitten to her cheek. "Did Maggie make it to Seattle okay?"

I nodded. "She had an appointment to meet with a doctor today. I have to admit I'm anxious to hear what he finds."

"She's going to be fine," Tara reassured me as a flock of seagulls noisily flew overhead, causing Max to jump up into the air as if he were trying to catch them.

"I hope you're right. It just doesn't seem like she should be sick for this long."

"How long will she be gone?" Tara asked.

"She's planning to come home on Monday, but I guess we'll see how it goes."

"And you're filling in at the Bait and Stitch?"

"Yeah, in the afternoons. I probably should think about going in and getting ready to go into town. I have to rework the whale watching tours for the weekend as well. Danny had a couple of large groups sign up for Saturday, so he's juggling the smaller groups to fit everyone in."

"I can do it," Tara offered. "I'm not busy today."

"Really? That would be great." Tara had helped out before and knew what to do. "I'll e-mail you the file. If you have questions just call Danny. I'll text him to let him know you're helping out. Thanks again."

"I'm happy to help. I turned in the proposal we reworked yesterday, so I'm free the rest of the week if you need me to fill in until Maggie gets back."

"That would be really helpful. The tourists from the mainland are starting to come over to see the whales now that they're back, and I know Danny's going to be swamped. I'm sure he'll really appreciate the help. How did the proposal turn out anyway?"

"I'm really happy with it. If you ask me, I think we have a good shot at making a go of this. I spoke to a couple of contractors who can start work as soon as we get loan approval. It'll be tight, but I think we can be open before the holidays. I've given this a lot of thought and I really believe if we . . ."

I looked out over the ocean as Tara rambled on. Most people wonder why we became friends in the first place. I love Tara like a sister, but even I have to admit that we're very different people. She's organized, calculating, and precise, and I'm disorganized, spontaneous, and casual to the point of sloppiness. Sometimes I think that her tendency toward obsessive control balances mine toward impulsivity and vice versa. Whatever the explanation for our bond, I know I'd be a lot worse off without her. Although I have two brothers and two sisters, Tara is as close to me as anyone.

"So what do you think?" Tara asked.

"Think?"

"Are you even listening to me?"

"Of course. You were talking about the cost of having all the supplies we'll need shipped over on a barge."

"Two topics ago. I've been talking about inventory control procedures for the past five minutes."

"I'm sure whatever you come up with will be fine."

"Don't you want to be part of the decision making?" Tara asked.

"Do I actually get to make any decisions?" I knew the real answer to this question was a resounding no, but Tara would never come right out and say so.

"Sure. We're a team," Tara assured me.

"Then I think we should paint the walls blue to match the sea." I pointed to a spot in the distance. "That blue, to be exact."

"I like blue," Tara agreed.

"See?" I smiled. "I'm helping, and as long as I'm helping, I'm going to head inside to get the box and litter you'll need."

"Box and litter?" Tara asked.

"For Bandit."

"Bandit?"

"That little charmer who stole your heart."

Tara looked down at the kitten, who had fallen asleep in her lap. "You think I should?"

"I do, and so does he."

By the time Max and I arrived at the Bait and Stitch the women's quilting circle was at full cackle. Again. Personally, I think the group does more gossiping than quilting.

Although many of the women who were present today were different from the ones who were there the previous day, the topic of conversation seemed to have picked up where it left off with Keith Weaver's death and its effect on the community as a whole. Most of the members of the circle were longtime residents who opposed the condo development. A good 90 percent of the women supported Maggie as candidate for the upcoming seat on the island council as well.

"Cait, your timing is perfect," Doris Rutherford, the self-appointed queen bee of the island gossip hotline, commented the moment I walked into the shop. "The girls and I were just discussing the special election."

"Special election?" I asked. I guess it made sense that they'd hold one to fill Keith's seat on the island council, but this was the first I'd heard of it. Of course, Irma Farmer, one of the other quilting regulars, lived next door to Mayor Bradley, who was also a member of the council. She was friendly with his wife, so she was often in the know about what was going on long before the general population.

"I would have thought Maggie would have been notified," Doris answered.

"She's in Seattle," I informed the group. "There may be a message on her answering machine. I forgot to check it this morning. So about this election . . . ?"

"Bill Powell is demanding that the council vote on his project in June, as originally planned. It's a well-known fact that the four remaining council members are split down the middle, which would result in a tie. The council decided to hold an emergency election to fill Keith's seat."

"Before June?"

"The election will be held the third Tuesday in June and the vote will take place at the council meeting in July," Irma confirmed. "I guess the council figured we already had four qualified candidates who've been campaigning for weeks to choose from, so why wait? Gary asked that they go ahead and fill his seat at this time as well, giving us four candidates for two seats."

I frowned. Gary Pixley already had been planning to retire from the council, but it seemed odd that he'd bail out early when there was such an important decision before the board. Gary opposed the development, which would surely send those members of the community who didn't want the condos to become a reality into a frenzy.

"Did he give a reason for dropping out early?" I asked.

"His hardware store has been struggling and the family plans to close up shop and leave the island," Irma said. "Maybe he saw the special election as a way to move up the timeline."

I considered the ramifications of this particular piece of news. Two seats of the five-member council were now open. Of the remaining three members, both Mayor Bradley and Grover Cloverdale were pro development, while one member, Byron Maxwell, was con. There were four candidates for the two seats. Both Aunt Maggie and Francine Rivers were con development, while Drake Moore and

Porter Wilson were pro. In order for the proposal to be defeated, Maggie and Francine would both have to win the special election and, conveniently, both of them were out of town. Coincidence? I thought not.

"Can the council even hold a special election on such short notice?" I said.

"I wondered the same thing myself," Doris answered. "I took a look at the bylaws, and unfortunately, they're very vague. Basically, the section relating to open seats in the middle of a term states that they can be filled by any means necessary in order to meet the needs of the council. Technically, they can simply appoint someone to fill Keith's position, which is what a couple of the members wanted to do, but there wasn't consensus on who should be appointed, thus the special election."

"Doesn't this all seem just a bit too coincidental?" I asked.

"How so?" Irma asked.

"Keith dies just prior to the vote, opening the door for not one but two pro development council members to be elected."

"You think someone killed Keith to sway the vote?" Irma asked.

"It's the only thing that makes sense."

"Personally, I would take a look at Keith's personal life over his role as a member of the island council," Doris commented.

"His personal life?" I asked.

"There's a rumor that Keith had been having an affair. Popular opinion is that he planned to leave his wife for this other woman."

"Keith has been having an affair? Where have I been?"

"That's the scuttlebutt," Doris confirmed.

I frowned. If Doris's piece of news was true, perhaps his wife had been the one to kill him. The thing was, if his wife was the killer, why do the deed in the old cannery? I knew Doris's tidbits could sometimes be nothing more than idle gossip, so I decided to remain focused on Keith's role in the upcoming vote and the impact his death would have on the outcome.

"Have you heard from Maggie?" Marley asked after she completed the transaction she'd been involved in when I'd come in and wandered across the store to join us.

"Not yet. I know Siobhan planned to take her to the doctor today. I hope one of them will call me when they know something, but if they don't, I'll call Siobhan at the apartment tonight."

Aunt Maggie refused to carry a cell phone, so calling her directly was impossible.

"I do hope they can figure out what's wrong," Marley fretted. "It's not like her to be down for so long."

"It seems like her symptoms began around the same time she decided to run for the island council," Doris said. "Do you think it could be stress that's making her ill? She's taken on a lot as of late."

"Maybe," the group agreed.

"What do you know about the new district manager for the bank?" I asked them. If anyone had the scoop on Camden Bradford, it would be this group.

"I know he isn't really a banker," Doris commented.

"What do you mean, he isn't really a banker?" I asked.

"Six months ago his brother-in-law was in a serious automobile accident," Doris shared. I had no idea where she got her information, but she generally tended to offer interesting tidbits. "The brother-in-law was the district manager at the bank before his accident, and although it appears he's going to be fine, his recovery has been slow. The bank was willing to keep his job open for a short time, but they were clear that if his injuries resulted in a prolonged absence they'd need to replace him. I guess Camden Bradford was some sort of high-profile investment banker before he quit and disappeared. The bank agreed to hold his brother-in-law's job indefinitely as long as he agreed to sub for him."

"What do you mean, he disappeared?" I asked.

Doris shrugged. "I'm not sure what he was doing, but it appears he quit his job a couple of years ago without any apparent reason, sold his penthouse apartment, and simply faded from society. He didn't reappear until after the accident."

"Why would the bank agree to let him fill in?" I wondered.

"I imagine they realized they were never going to get anyone even half as qualified as he is for the money they were offering," Doris theorized.

"I heard that Bradford's brother-in-law is close to returning to work," Ruth offered. "So Camden Bradford will probably disappear from the island as abruptly as he appeared."

My phone rang. I looked at the caller ID. "It's Siobhan," I commented before answering.

The group whispered quietly as I spoke to my sister. I could see that Marley was almost as tense as I was as she waited to hear the fate of her best friend in the entire world. I don't know what I was expecting Siobhan to report, but of all the things I anticipated might be wrong with Maggie, the truth was so much worse than I feared.

After we finished at the Bait and Stitch for the day, Max and I decided to head over to the marina to see if Danny was around. When I arrived at the boat, Danny and Tara were sitting on the deck of his boat enjoying a beer with Cody. I almost turned around and left, but everyone had seen me and I didn't want to seem pathetic. Danny handed me a bottle as I sat down across from the group.

"It's nice to see you, Cait." I tried not to look at Cody, who looked even better than I remembered him. I'd managed a brief glance at him when he'd come by with Danny to fix the screen, but I'd been so terrified about being caught in just a towel that I hadn't taken the time to really appreciate the way he'd filled out.

"I heard you're on the island for the whole summer," I said.

"I'm about to finish my tour with the Navy and am trying to decide whether to re-up or move on to something else. I had some leave coming, so I decided to come back to the island to think things through."

"I'm surprised you'd come here," I said snottily. "Now that your parents have moved, I can't see that there's a lot for you on Madrona."

"I have friends."

"Good friends." Danny shot me a look. "Cody was just telling us about his time with the Seals. It's really fascinating."

"I'm sure it is. I heard from Siobhan," I changed the subject in an abrupt manner that I was certain didn't present me in the best light. I thought both Danny and Tara understood how much Cody had hurt me, but here they were, chatting with him like he was the best thing since sliced bread.

"And?" Danny asked. I knew he was as anxious about Maggie's health as I was.

"According to the lab results, Maggie has a significant amount of arsenic in her system. Not enough to kill her; just enough to make her sick."

"Arsenic?" Danny frowned. "How on earth did she get arsenic poisoning?"

"Siobhan said that someone has to be slipping it to her. Probably in her food."

"That sounds like it could be serious," Cody added.

"Yes, I imagine it is," I replied.

"So the person would have to have access to her food. Other than you, who could that possibly be?" Tara wondered.

"I'm not really sure," I admitted. "Maggie doesn't eat out often, so chances are that the food in the house is somehow being contaminated."

"You've been cooking for Maggie and eating at her house most nights since she's been sick," Tara pointed out, "yet you seem to feel just fine."

"That's true," I agreed. "If the food in Maggie's kitchen was contaminated I should be sick as well. Whatever it is that's making her sick, it must be something only she eats or drinks."

"Maybe she's coming into contact with the substance at the store," Danny suggested. "One of the regulars could be slipping the poison into her food when she isn't looking."

I frowned. "Who would do that?"

"I don't know, but someone obviously is."

Danny was right; someone was slipping the poison into her food and I knew it wasn't me.

"Okay, let's say it's true. Other than the three of us, who does Maggie come into contact with on a regular basis?" I asked.

"Maggie spends more time with Marley than anyone else," Tara began.

"Yeah, but there's no way Marley would hurt Maggie." Maggie and Marley had been best friends since they were young girls. Sure, they argued at times, but everyone knew they cared deeply about each other.

"The ladies from the quilting circle seem to spend an awful lot of time at the Bait and Stitch," Danny began.

"Yeah," I admitted reluctantly, "but I really can't see any of them hurting her. What possible reason could they have for doing so?"

"What possible reason could *anyone* have for doing so?" Danny asked. "Maggie is opinionated and outspoken, but someone is *poisoning* her. It takes a real wacko to do something like that."

"Or someone with a really good motive," Tara inserted.

"Whoever is doing it must have at least a rudimentary knowledge of the poison and how it works," Cody pointed out. "If not, she'd most likely be dead by now."

Cody had a point. Someone had made sure that Maggie would become sick, but not too sick. I paused to think about the situation. The nearly full moon was reflecting off the water, which most times brought a sense of peace and contentment to my troubled thoughts. But not tonight. Tonight I was filled with fear for Maggie. Someone seemed to want her out of the way, though not necessarily dead.

"I'm going to go out on a limb and say that whoever killed Keith is also responsible for poisoning Maggie," I stated.

"So we're looking for someone who has access to Maggie's food and also has access to the old cannery," Danny summarized.

Not a single person came to mind. Camden Bradford had access to the cannery, but he certainly didn't have access to Maggie's food. Other than myself, Marley had the most access to Maggie's food, but there was no way either of us did it. Something wasn't adding up. I looked across the marina to see Tansy walking toward us with Romeo trotting along behind. Tansy lived nearby, but what in the heck was Romeo doing all the way over here? When I'd left home that morning he'd been safely locked in the cabin.

"It looks like Tansy found my vagabond cat," I announced. "I'll be back in a minute."

I got up from my seat and hopped up onto the dock. It was a short walk down the wooden walkway to where Tansy was waiting.

"Where ever did you find Romeo?" I asked after giving the woman a quick hug.

"He came for me."

"He came for you?"

"He knew you needed a nudge."

"A nudge?" I asked.

"He wanted me to warn you about the tea."

"The tea?" I remembered Romeo knocking Maggie's cup of tea off the counter the previous morning. Maggie was the only one who ever drank the bitter brew.

"I need to call Finn." I hugged Tansy. "Thank you so much. It makes perfect sense."

"Don't thank me; thank Romeo."

Tansy bent down and picked up the cat. She gave him a scratch under his chin before handing him to me.

"I should go," she informed me. She turned to walk away, then paused and turned back. "Just remember that things often are exactly what they seem."

With that, she faded into the darkness.

I'd never been able to figure out how she managed that particular trick. I cuddled Romeo to my chest and headed back to the boat. My new plan for the evening was to call Finn and turn over the tea for testing, after which I'd head home and lie awake all night trying to figure out what Tansy's last comment meant.

Chapter 11

Friday, May 22

The next morning I decided to pay a visit to Kim Darby. She'd been Keith Weaver's receptionist for a number of years, and if anyone knew what was going on with the man prior to his murder, it would be her. Although Keith ran a one-man office, which would now be forced to close, Kim had kept the doors open temporarily to aid in the transfer of his clients to fellow Realtor Porter Wilson. As I hoped, she was sitting at her desk in the front office when I arrived at Weaver Real Estate.

Although Keith ran a small business, he was very successful in his endeavors, and his office was furnished to demonstrate that fact. While Porter Wilson's office tended toward the tawdry, Keith provided clients with cherrywood tables, comfortable chairs, and expensive artwork to gaze upon while they filled out the mountains of paperwork demanded by each transaction. I greeted Kim and sat down in one of the soft leather chairs.

"How are you holding up?" I asked the obviously overworked woman.

"It's been a struggle," Kim admitted. "Not only am I trying to deal with the loss of a good friend but I've been swamped trying to transfer all of Keith's clients over to Porter. Most of them aren't happy with the change, but there really aren't a lot of options on the island."

Kim had a point. Other than Porter Wilson, the only other Realtor on the island was a man named Davenport who dealt exclusively with high-end clients.

"I know how busy you must be and I don't want to take up a lot of your time, but I was wondering about a comment Tara made just before we found Keith's body. She said you'd shared with her the fact that Keith was planning not only to support Bill Powell's development but that he was going to push it through the council. It was my understanding he was very much against the project."

"He was, at first," Kim confirmed. "In fact, he put a lot of time into gathering facts to use to support his arguments against the project. Then several weeks ago he told me he'd changed his mind and had decided to support it. I was as surprised as anyone. The thing is," Kim hesitated, "I overheard a phone conversation on the day before his body was found. He mentioned that he'd made a deal with the devil and wasn't sure how he was going to get out of it."

I frowned. "A deal with the devil? Do you have any idea what he was talking about?"

"Not really. I'd talk to Bill Powell, though. He seems to have gained the most by Keith's death; other than Porter Wilson, of course, who now has a virtual monopoly on the island as far as real estate is concerned."

I knew that not only was Porter Wilson the only other Realtor on the island who took walk-in clients but he was also running for island council and openly supported Bill's project. It seemed the two men were isolated at the top of the suspect list.

"Can you think of anyone else who might have a motive for wanting Keith dead?" I asked.

"No, not a single person. Everyone loved Keith."

"I heard through the grapevine that Keith was having an affair and planned to leave his wife."

"What?" Kim seemed shocked by the idea. "I know Keith's wife is a total witch, and he had made hints that he might have no choice but to end things, but Keith would never cheat. I think your source has been misinformed."

"Yeah, you're probably right. Thanks for your time."

I had promised Mr. Parsons I would return on Friday, and I really wanted to make sure things with Rambler were still going okay, so I stopped by the grocery store to restock his pantry, then stopped by my cabin to pick up Max. By the time we arrived at Mr. Parsons's estate it was almost noon. I'd told Marley I'd help out at the Bait and Stitch that afternoon, so it was going to have to be a short visit.

When I walked into the house after being buzzed in by Mr. Parsons I found the man sitting in the study with Banjo and Summer, a hippie couple in their late sixties who lived in a small shack down the beach. The group were watching what appeared to be a rerun of an old soap opera. Max jogged over to join Rambler, who was happily watching from his spot on the sofa.

"Cait, how are you, dear?" Banjo got up, gave me a hug, and kissed me square on the lips.

"I'm fine. It's been a few weeks. How's the shop doing?"

Banjo and Summer owned an eclectic shop in Pelican Bay that sold a variety of random items. It was located next to Herbalities, the shop that was owned by Bella and Tansy. They had an excellent location, right on the harbor; the problem was they only seemed to be open when the mood struck them. Here it was midday on a Friday and they were watching reruns with Mr. Parsons.

Still, their lifestyle seemed to suit them. They'd never married or had children, but they'd traveled widely and never seemed stressed about anything. There were times when I had to admire their ability to take things as they came and never fight the current.

"It's doin'." Banjo shrugged. "Summer has some new pottery to display and I've been working on my tie-dyed T-shirts. I'm experimenting with new color combinations."

"Shh," Summer admonished. "We're almost to the part where they find out that Dirk's third son is really not his son but his brother."

I had to suppress a giggle. The premise sounded ridiculous, but Summer seemed totally into the show, as did the others.

"I picked up a few things for your pantry when I was at the store. I'll put them away and then come back to visit with you for a while. Can you keep an eye on Max for me?"

"I'd be happy to, dear." Mr. Parsons smiled. "If you hurry you can catch the end, where we find out that Dirk's twin brother isn't really dead, as everyone believes. It turns out he faked his own death and ran away with Dirk's wife, who disappeared without a trace over a year ago. It's going to throw the whole town into a tizzy."

"I'll hurry," I promised.

I was pleasantly surprised to see that Mr. Parsons's living space was tidier than it had been for quite a while. Maybe having Rambler to keep him company had given him a new lease on life. I put the groceries away and made a quick check to see if there were any dishes that needed tending to, but everything looked spotlessly clean. I smiled as I made my way back to the study. The trio were completely engrossed in the show and didn't even look up when I walked up behind them. I couldn't help but chuckle when all three television viewers gasped in surprise when Dirk's twin walked into the room, dressed in nothing but a very small towel. I had to admit that the actor who played both Dirk and his twin was quite the babe. Suddenly, I realized why Summer was glued to the show, but I didn't understand the fascination Banjo and Mr. Parsons seemed to share.

"I can't believe Dirk didn't deck the guy," Mr. Parsons commented as Dirk's brother revealed his whereabouts for the past year.

"I think the poor man is in shock," Summer sympathized.

"He's probably afraid the towel the guy's wearing will fall off if he hits him," Banjo contributed. "Besides, after the upset with his son, I bet the man isn't sure what to believe."

The group let out a sigh as the show ended and the credits began to roll across the screen.

"Is this a new show?" I asked when I decided it was safe to speak.

"No, it's a soap from the sixties," Summer answered. "Banjo and I don't have a television, so we come over to watch reruns with Mr. Parsons."

"It seems like you must have seen these episodes before," I commented.

"Oh, dozens of times. This show is one of our favorites. It seems like everyone is having an affair with everyone else, and I do so love a juicy affair."

"Speaking of affairs, have any of you heard anything about Keith Weaver having been involved in one prior to his death?"

"Oh, I'm certain of it," Banjo answered.

"Really? Did he mention it to you?"

"No. He didn't say anything," Banjo told me, "but I could tell he had a thing on the side, with all the strutting around he'd been doing. If I had to guess, I'd say it ended just before he was murdered. He seemed to have lost the spring in his step."

"Do you know who the affair was with?" I asked.

"He didn't say and I didn't ask."

"This is just like one of our stories." Summer grinned. "I bet it was the wife who offed him. Or maybe the lover."

"Can't see killin' a man over some messy love affair," Banjo countered. "My money is on Bill Powell, or someone associated with his project."

"It would seem that greed would trump jealousy as a motive," Mr. Parsons agreed. "Although," he added, "the best motive of all is revenge."

"Revenge?" I asked. "Do you think someone had a grudge against Keith Weaver?"

Summer laughed. "It sounds like a lot of people had reason to hold a grudge against the man. His wife, if she found out about the affair; the lover, if he broke it off; the people who would have been affected by his decision to back the condo project, to name a few."

"So you also heard he'd changed his mind about blocking the project?" I asked.

"Yeah, he told us himself that he'd decided to support it," Summer confirmed.

"He knew Summer and I were concerned about the impact of the project on our own property values; the land they planned to build on borders ours," Banjo added.

I really hadn't considered that, but Banjo was correct. The new building would definitely impact the isolation the couple now enjoyed.

"When did he tell you this?" I asked.

"'Bout a week ago," Banjo answered. "He came by for some of Summer's special cookies"—I knew marijuana was the special ingredient in Summer's cookies— "and he confessed to his change of heart. He seemed to feel bad about it. He knew how much we were counting on his support when it came time to vote on the project."

"Kim made it sound like he might have been having second thoughts about that decision," I commented.

"If he was, he didn't mention it to us," Summer verified.

I paused to consider the situation. Keith Weaver had initially been very vocal in his opposition to the project. And then, for some unknown reason that seemed to have to do with a deal with the devil, he changed his mind. It seemed as if he might have changed his mind yet again before he died. All the evidence at this point seemed to support the fact that one of these decision changes might have led to his death.

By the time I got home that day it was close to dark. It seemed like the afternoon had dragged on and on. Not that it isn't usually fun to help out at the Bait and Stitch, but today my mind was filled with suspects, motives, and opportunity. Now that I knew that someone had intentionally been poisoning Maggie, I was more determined than ever to unmask the killer.

"Romeo," I called after Max and I had settled the groceries I'd picked up into the kitchen. It was odd that he hadn't come to the door when I'd walked in. "I brought salmon treats," I said persuasively.

When that didn't bring him running I realized the sly little feline had most likely slipped out of the cabin once again. At least Francine was still out of town. I gave Max his dinner, put on a jacket, and headed around the hedge to the next house. I understand the draw of new love, but Romeo really was going to create a difficult situation for both of us if he didn't find a way to curb his lusty feelings for Juliet.

I was just about to turn inland from the beach and approach Francine's back lawn when I literally ran into none other than Camden Bradford.

"Juliet?" I asked.

"How'd you know?"

"I'm missing Romeo as well. I figured the pair must have snuck away for a romantic interlude."

"I don't suppose Romeo is neutered?"

"'Fraid not. I plan to have it done, but he's really only been with me for a few days. How about Juliet?"

"No. Francine was hoping to have her bred to another show cat."

I had a bad feeling about this. A very bad feeling. Francine wasn't going to be happy if Romeo and Juliet decided to consummate their obvious affection for each other. "We need to find them. And fast."

"Any idea where to look?" Cam asked.

I looked around the surrounding area. They could be anywhere by this point.

Romeo had seemed fascinated by Mr. Parsons's garden when we'd taken a walk down the beach earlier in the week. "Let's head down the beach to see what we find. I'm sure they'll come home on their own; what I'm afraid of is what Juliet's state of chastity will be by then."

I turned and began walking toward Mr. Parsons's property and Cam fell in next to me. It really was a beautiful evening: warmer than it had been, and the tide was in, creating gentle waves that lapped onto the shore. The moon, which had been nearly full the previous evening, was just beginning its ascent from the east. While technically none of the beaches on Madrona Island were private, the isolation of the small peninsula where Maggie lived provided an element of solitude. Occasionally we got boaters who would pull up onto the sand during the peak of the summer, but for most of the year this particular stretch of sand was deserted.

"Have you lived on the island long?" Cam asked conversationally as we walked down the sand.

"All my life."

"It really is one of the most beautiful places I've ever been, and I've been a lot of places."

"Have you ever thought of settling here?"

"Actually, the thought has crossed my mind."

"I heard you're just filling in temporarily at the bank."

Cam looked surprised that I knew that. "Everyone really does know everyone else's business on the island."

"It's a byproduct of living in such an isolated social situation," I confirmed.

"And you heard about my brother-in-law as well?"

"I have. It's really nice what you're doing for him."

Cam shrugged. "I'm a nice guy. Besides, I love my sister. I'd do anything for her, and my brother-in-law really needs this job."

"How much longer do you think you'll be needed at the bank?"

"Not long. If everything works out as planned, my last day should be June 30, which happens to be my birthday. I think birthdays are a perfect time for new beginnings."

"And then?"

Cam frowned. "I'm not sure. I'd been doing some traveling, but to be honest, by the time the accident occurred I was pretty much ready to come back to the States and find a new career. I hadn't decided what exactly that might entail, but I find that I'd really like to try something new. I guess once I'm no longer needed at the bank I'll have to give it some thought."

I realized that the fact that Cam had made a lot of money early in his career explained his superexpensive car. If he could afford to take two years off he must have made a lot of money. I tried to remember if I knew the previous district manager for the bank because that must be Cam's brother-in-law. I'd never had to borrow money until last winter, so it was doubtful I'd ever met the man.

"Oh, look," I whispered. Romeo and Juliet were both in Mr. Parsons's garden, as I'd suspected they would be. Juliet was sitting up on a bench and Romeo was sitting on the ground next to her, reaching his paw toward her.

"Aren't they adorable?" I added. "It seems a shame to interrupt."

"Yeah, it does, but Francine will kill us if Juliet ends up pregnant with a tomcat's babies. We'd better break them up before it's too late."

"I guess we should," I reluctantly agreed.

Luckily, both cats stayed put as we approached. I picked up Romeo and Cam picked up Juliet and we headed back down the beach.

When I returned home Cody was sitting on my front deck. As much as I hoped we could avoid each other for the duration of his stay, deep down I knew it most likely wouldn't be so.

"What are you doing here?" I asked.

"I thought we should chat."

"So chat." I opened the front door and motioned for Cody to precede Romeo and me inside.

Cody sat down on the sofa while I tossed another log on the fire. Although spring had arrived, it was still cool in the evenings.

"Who's the guy?" Cody asked. He must have seen me walking down the beach with Cam. We'd each been carrying a cat. I'm sure it looked very romantic.

"My boyfriend," I lied. "So why are you here?"

"I could tell by your complete avoidance of eye contact when we ran into each other on Danny's boat that you're less than thrilled that I'm spending time on the island. We've always been friends. What happened was unfortunate, but I hate to see it ruin our friendship."

"What friendship? You took my virginity and then you left."

"I know. It was a mistake. A huge mistake. I never meant for things to progress that far. I really have no excuse for what happened except to say that I'd been attracted to you for a long time, and you seemed so willing. It was a bad decision that I've regretted every day since."

"You were attracted to me?" I couldn't quite believe that.

"I was."

"Yet you left."

"What was I supposed to do?" Cody asked. "I'd already enlisted in the Navy. I had plane tickets for the next day. I had to go."

I guess Cody had a point. Sixteen-year-old Caitlin had been so wrapped up in irrational teenage emotions that she couldn't see that she was as much if not more to blame for the situation than Cody was. If the same thing happened today I would have handled it differently.

"I sent you a letter as soon as I got settled," he pointed out.

"A letter of apology. Do you know how it made me feel that you considered the most amazing night of my life to be some huge mistake?"

"The most amazing night of your life?" Cody grinned.

"Don't flatter yourself. I had no means of comparison at that point. At best it was passable."

I hoped my nose wouldn't grow with all the lies I was telling. I still considered my night with Cody, in spite of everything that happened after, to be the best I'd ever had.

"I'm sorry," Cody said, his voice sincere. "I handled it badly. That night was amazing, but the fact that I had to leave made it so much harder."

"Yeah, I guess I can see that. So why did you stay away so long? It's been ten years."

Cody shrugged. "I don't know. That first tour was hard, but it gave me a sense of purpose. I was doing something important. Making a difference. And then I was accepted into the Seal program and my life trajectory seemed set. I'm not even sure why I'm hesitating to re-up now, except that I'm starting to consider everything I'm missing."

"Missing?" I asked.

"A wife. A family. Friends with whom I share a history."

I just looked at this man I did *not* want to love. Deep inside, I knew that in the end he'd leave again. If I opened my heart to him I'd get hurt, and this time I wasn't sure there was any coming back.

"I'd like us to be friends again," Cody added. "I want to have people in my life who know about the intimate details of my past."

"Intimate details?" I asked.

"Okay, maybe intimate isn't the right word. But, other than my family, the people living on this island are the only people I share childhood memories with. They're the only ones who know that I was the shortest kid in my class until the ninth grade, and that I threw the winning touchdown at the state championship when I was a junior, and that I dressed as Superman for Halloween three years in a row."

"And that those three years happened to be when you were in high school," I reminded him with a laugh.

"See." Cody grinned. "I can't share that embarrassing fact with a single person outside of the residents of Madrona Island and not come off as some huge geek."

"You are a huge geek."

Cody shrugged. "Maybe. But I'm a geek who knows all of your most embarrassing memories as well. I guess that puts us on equal ground. So how about it?"

"I don't know. I'll have to think about it."

Cody stood up. "Fair enough. I'll see you around."

Chapter 12

Sunday, May 24

There are some things you should never agree to do even for your favorite brother. Going on a blind date with someone neither of you has ever met, it turns out, is one of them. By the time Saturday evening rolled around I was pretty much regretting my decision to spend the evening with Danny, his date, and her cousin. When the pair of men showed up at my door, I found that I regretted the decision even more.

How can I describe Melanie's cousin Walter? The word nerd comes to mind, but that would be too kind. Nerd with a superiority complex and deep emotional issues would be a bit closer. Don't get me wrong; I'm not a snob and every guy I date doesn't need to be a perfect 10, but Walter was . . . well, Walter was a truly unique individual.

"You're slouching," Mom reminded me as I stood in front of her refrigerator in my bare feet the day after the disastrous date.

I stood up straight. My mom was a wonderful woman, but she was a stickler for proper posture.

"Is the salami I saw in here earlier gone?" I asked.

"It's in the deli drawer, but it's much too late to be having a snack. Dinner will be ready in an hour."

"But I'm hungry now," I argued. Why is it that anytime I visit my childhood home I turn back into a petulant child?

"You can snack on a carrot while you shred the lettuce for the salad."

I grabbed the bag of carrots as well as the head of lettuce from the crisper and headed toward the cutting board, which was already set out on the kitchen counter. If I'd been at my own home I would have stuffed my mouth with cookies just to prove I could.

"Have you given any more thought to helping out with the children's choir?" Mom asked.

The woman who had led the choir for the past twenty years had left the island and the church was looking for a replacement. Unfortunately, I had a passable voice, and Mom had suggested to Father Kilian that I might make an acceptable replacement.

"I don't know. It seems like a big commitment."

"You'd just have Wednesday night practice and Sunday morning services. Sister Mary really needs you to do this."

I sincerely doubted that, since Sister Mary seemed quite adept at recruiting volunteers to help out with the children's programs she was in charge of, but spending time with the kids would be fun, and I really wasn't busy on Wednesday evenings.

"Okay, I'll give it a try," I agreed.

"Wonderful." Mom smiled. "I thought today's sermon might have made an impact. It was a perfect time for Father Kilian to discuss service to the community," Mom continued to drone on. "It seems like he has a knack for knowing just what message to share at the most appropriate time. Don't you think?"

"Um," I answered as I let my mind drift to last night's date. If I knew my mom, and I did, she'd spend the next twenty minutes providing examples of Father Kilian's knack for delivering the perfect message at the perfect time.

The evening had started out okay. Danny had made reservations at the best restaurant on the island, which helped to make the situation palatable. The Sea

Grotto, an oceanfront restaurant best known for serving seafood that had been caught the same day it was served, is perched high on a bluff that overlooks a rocky seashore. On a clear night the lights from both the Canadian mainland and Vancouver Island can be seen from the windows that look out over the Pacific Ocean. It really is the perfect choice for a romantic evening.

Unfortunately, the date disintegrated the moment we sat down. Walter was as rude as any man I'd ever met. I spent a lot of time looking out those windows as I tried to ignore the condescending way the jerk spoke to the wait staff. It totally amazed me that Danny's date, Melanie, put up with his nonsense. Melanie is a cocktail waitress at a local bar, yet she seemed to encourage rather than discourage Walter's abuse of the perfectly nice men and women who served our fifty-dollar-a-plate meals.

"Cait?" my mom asked.

I looked up at the slightly plump woman who was still dressed in the knee-length dress she'd worn to Mass. If you ask me, trying to cook a big family dinner while still dressed in your Sunday finest was ridiculous, but Mom insisted that all the Hart women wear dresses or skirts on Sunday.

"I think the lettuce is small enough," Mom added.

I looked down to see that I had shredded the leafy greens into microscopic pieces while I indulged on my rant down memory lane.

"Sorry." I pushed the bowl aside and started dicing tomatoes.

"Is there something on your mind?"

My first instinct was to shrug. I had grown up sitting at this very counter helping Mom with the cooking and it had become firmly engrained in my psyche that the teenage code of conduct required that you never volunteered information to a parent even if you secretly wanted to share it with them. I'm not really sure how this particular rule came into being, but I can say that I'd become a master at making my poor mother pry every little bit of information out of me. Of course, now I was twenty-six, not sixteen, so perhaps it was time to grow up and learn the art of adult conversation.

"I went on a double date with Danny last night," I began.

"And?" Mom prodded.

"And the guy was a real douche."

"Caitlin Hart, we do not say 'douche' in this household. Now you go into the bedroom and say five Hail Marys."

So much for adult conversation.

I shoved the tomatoes aside and did as I was instructed. The Hart family had not only been Catholic for dozens of generations but we were very conservative Irish Catholic. Don't get me wrong; I'm proud of my heritage and my religion, but at times strict adherence to the old ways can become tiring.

As an adult, I live in a world made up of boxes. There's the Sunday box, which I think of as my Harthaven box. It includes the village of Harthaven, my mother, the church, and the mandatory Sunday dinner every Hart on the island is required to attend. While I'd had a wonderful childhood filled with love and fond memories, there's a part of me that longs for something more than can be experienced in this blue collar environment, where hard work, family, church, and tradition, are the cornerstones of everyday life.

During the other six days of the week I live in Pelican Bay, a modern town with eclectic residents that was built on the idea of personal enrichment, spiritual freedom, and economic prosperity. In

Pelican Bay I share my life with wonderfully free-spirited souls, including two witches, hippie neighbors, and a cat who apparently has some sort of magical powers.

Aunt Maggie is my role model. Of all the people I know, she seems most adept at straddling the line between these two very different worlds. Sure, she's politically opinionated and tends to ruffle feathers along the way, but she has a unique understanding of what it means not only to live in, but fully embrace, each of these very different cultures.

"So what did you get busted for?" My sixteen-year-old sister Cassidy asked when she joined me in the bedroom.

"Saying douche."

Cassidy laughed. "Did it get you out of making dinner?"

"Actually, it did." I smiled.

"It seems sort of pointless to even make a big dinner today." Cassie plopped down on the bed. "Aunt Maggie is still at Siobhan's, Aiden is in Alaska getting the boat ready for the season, and Danny called to say he was sick."

"More like hung over. I wish I'd thought of calling in sick."

"If you had, maybe Mom would have let me go hang out with my friends."

"You know that Sunday is family day."

"What family? At least when you were my age the aunts and uncles and cousins used to come over. Now it's just us and so, so boring." Cassie groaned and covered her eyes with her forearm. "No one has known pain like I have."

Did I mention that Cassie tends to be somewhat melodramatic? Yet she did have a point. Things had changed quite a lot since I was sixteen. Dad was still alive then, and Aiden and Siobhan were always around. The island was still home to most of my dad's siblings and their families. Sunday dinner meant dozens of people who shared a bloodline and would come together to share a meal. The boys would throw a ball around in the yard, while the men drank beer and the women gossiped about who needed to make a trip to the confessional right away and who could probably get by with waiting another week.

In the span of the ten years between my sixteenth and my twenty-sixth year, my dad had died, the cannery had closed, Siobhan had moved to Seattle, and all of the Hart aunts and uncles, other than Maggie, had moved from the island. What was once a chorus of voices was now but an echo of what had once been.

"I thought Tara was coming for dinner," Cassie added.

"She was, but she stayed to help Sister Mary with the plans for the program they're offering to the children this summer. Maybe we should see if Mom wants to go out to dinner. My treat," I offered.

"She's already made the stew."

"It'll keep."

"I guess it couldn't hurt to ask." Cassie smiled.

Luckily, Mom hadn't started the bread or the potatoes, and even she had to agree that a big family dinner for the three of us was just short of depressing. Many of the businesses in Harthaven were closed on Sundays, but if you liked Italian food there was always an open table at Antonio's, where parishioners of St. Patrick's often congregated to share a meal and catch up with their neighbors.

We paused after walking in as Mom scanned the room, looking for an empty table. The crowded restaurant featured red-and-white-checked tablecloths, thick white candles that dripped over the side of repurposed wine bottles, and colorful baskets of red and white flowers. I took an appreciative breath as the scent of garlic and spicy tomato sauce transported me back to similar meals from my childhood.

"Oh, look, some of the members of my prayer group are sitting at the big table in the back," Mom announced as we walked in through the front door. "Why don't we join them?"

I could see Cassie was about to complain, but I squeezed her hand just in time to prevent an outburst.

"I think there are only two seats available," I said. "Why don't you go ahead, and Cassie and I will sit at the empty table in the corner."

Mom frowned. "Are you sure?"

"Absolutely. That's okay with you?" I looked at Cassie.

She smiled. "Yeah, that's fine. I wanted to talk to Cait about the new computer software program I'm thinking of downloading."

That was a smart move on Cassie's part because Mom hated everything computer related.

"Okay, if you're sure." Mom looked back toward the table where her friends were congregated. I noticed her eyes had locked on the empty chair next to a man the family had known since before I was born who happened to be a recent widower. "Maybe I'll join the two of you for dessert."

"That would be nice," I agreed.

The table Cassie and I headed to was just to the right of the red-brick fireplace that smoldered with red coals as the fire burned down.

"Is there anything going on between Mom and Mr. O'Donnell?" I asked as I sat across from Cassie.

"What? Ew! Why would you even ask that?"

"I noticed her noticing him when we walked in. It *has* been three years since Dad passed and two years since Mrs. O'Donnell passed. I just thought . . ."

"Well, unthink it. Mr. O'Donnell is too old for Mom. Besides, they're both too old to be dating anyone."

I sincerely doubted that either Mom or Mr. O'Donnell were too old to date but decided to let the subject drop. "So how about you? I think you mentioned a new guy. Justin?"

A dreamy look came over Cassie's face. "Justin is awesome. He's smart and athletic and a total babe. We aren't actually boyfriend and girlfriend, but we've been out a few times, so unless Mom blows it for me, I'm hoping to take the next step."

"Why do you think Mom would blow your chance with this guy?" I wondered.

"Justin is eighteen. He's not used to dating girls with ten o'clock curfews. In fact, I'm pretty sure the other girls he dates don't even have curfews. I've tried to get Mom to lighten up, but she refuses to be even a tiny bit reasonable."

"To be honest, I'm surprised she's letting you date someone who's eighteen at all."

"She doesn't exactly know he's eighteen," Cassie admitted. "I told her that he was a junior, which he is, but she isn't aware that he was held back a couple of times."

"So next year when he's a senior he'll be nineteen?"

Cassie shrugged. "Justin's thinking about dropping out after this year. He would have done it already, but his parents told him that if he dropped out he would need to move out of their house, so he's hanging in until one of the jobs he's applied for comes through. It'll be so awesome if he can get his own place."

I found myself in one of those moments when I wanted to pause the scene so I had time to think things through. There was no way I wanted my baby sister dating an adult with his own place, but I knew if I turned all parental on her, she'd simply shut me out. I wanted her to know she could come to me any time about anything and I would be there to listen and offer support. Siobhan had filled that role for me and I intended to fill it for Cassie.

I was formulating the perfect big sister response when Camden Bradford walked in with Bill Powell. He waved when he saw me and started across the restaurant in our direction. I could feel my stomach churn as I considered the fact that the two men I most suspected in Keith Weaver's murder had shown up at one of the most popular restaurants in Harthaven together.

"Cait, so nice to see you. Do you know Bill Powell?" Camden introduced us.

"We've met," I confirmed. "This is my sister Cassie."

"Nice to meet you."

Cassie turned a bright red when Cam shook her hand. "It's nice to meet you too," Cassie stammered.

"So what brings you to the Catholic side of town?" I asked, admittedly somewhat rudely.

"Church, actually," Cam answered. "I was coming out of the afternoon service when I ran into Bill, and we decided to grab a bite."

"You're Catholic?" I asked.

"Born and raised. You seem surprised."

I wanted to say I was surprised that a churchgoing man would commit a cruel and senseless murder, but then again, churchgoing men commit cruel and senseless murders every day.

Okay, let me stop here and say that I really have no idea why I won't let go of the idea that Camden Bradford is guilty of killing Keith Weaver. He actually seems like a perfectly lovely man. And he had been really nice when we'd gone looking for the cats on Friday evening. There was just something about him that caused my stomach to knot up whenever he was around.

"It looks like our table is ready," Bill said, just in time to save me from making a response.

The men said their good-byes before turning to cross the restaurant.

"Who was that?" Cassie breathed.

"New district manager for the bank."

"Are you dating?"

"Of course we aren't dating. I barely know the man."

"It seemed like he was giving you the look."

"What look?" I asked.

"You know. The look."

"Can we get back to this much-too-old boyfriend of yours?"

Cassie took a sip of her water. "It's interesting how you're so intent on discussing my love life, but when it comes to yours . . ."

"I don't have a love life."

"Exactly."

Cassie had a point in that there was something about Camden Bradford that caused my nerve endings to sizzle. The thing was, I really couldn't tell if what I was feeling was attraction or a sixth sense that was warning me that the guy wasn't as nice as he appeared to be. There was something about him that I couldn't bring myself to trust.

After Cassie and I ordered lasagna with garlic bread and garden salads, we allowed the conversation to gravitate toward less sticky subjects than our love lives. While I worried about Cassie's choice of love interest, I knew there wasn't a thing I could do about it. Cassie was the independent sort who wasn't apt to take advice from me or anyone else.

"So what's going on with your murder investigation?" Cassie asked.

"What makes you think I'm investigating a murder?" I asked.

"Kourtney Darby told me that she overheard her mother telling someone that you'd been digging around, trying to turn up information on Keith Weaver's murder."

"Did Kourtney mention who her mother was speaking to?"

"She didn't know. Her mom was on the phone and she changed the subject when she noticed Kourtney was listening in. Kourtney said her mom was pretty mad about it, although she also said her mom was pretty mad about almost everything since her dad left."

"Kim and her husband are separated?" I hadn't known that.

"Kourtney said her mom and dad had a fight, then her dad went totally ballistic, took his stuff, and split without even saying good-bye."

"That's too bad. I hope they work it out."

"Kourtney is pretty worried about the situation. I guess her dad has been in trouble before for beating up some guy. She said the other guy totally deserved it, but her dad still ended up spending a couple of months in the slammer. Kourtney said her dad is a good guy when he hasn't been drinking and hopes he'll manage to keep his cool until he calms down a bit."

"He doesn't sound like the sort of guy Kourtney should be living with," I observed as the waitress set our salads and a basket of golden garlic bread on the table.

"Kourt told me her mom's temper is even worse than her dad's. They met at some kind of court-mandated anger management class. Talk about a wacky way to meet the person you're going to marry."

Chapter 13

Monday, May 25

Today was Memorial Day. While the schools were out and the bank was closed, this particular day of the year varied only slightly from any other Monday in Pelican Bay. The town was built around the idea of commerce. Danny was booked with whale watching tours and the Bait and Stitch was open to meet the needs of holiday visitors. The main street, which runs along the harbor, features a variety of eclectic shops and restaurants, including Herbalities (Bella and Tansy's store), Ship Wreck (Banjo and Summer's place), Off the Hook (a sushi bar), and For the Halibut (a fish market), and on this busy Monday the shops were crowded with day trippers from the mainland out to enjoy the warm spring holiday.

Maggie called to let me know she would be staying with Siobhan a few more days to rest up before her trip back to the island. I felt torn about her decision. On one hand, I wanted my aunt to get the rest she needed in order to experience a complete recovery; on the other, I worried that her absence might affect not only the upcoming election but the quality of life on Madrona Island in the future.

Tara was helping Danny for the day and Marley seemed to be doing okay on her own when I stopped by, so I decided to take an hour to follow up on a hunch that had been lingering in the back of my mind for several days.

It seemed to me that there were several things going on that on the surface seemed to have nothing to do with one another but my intuition told me had to be related.

First of all, there was Keith Weaver's murder. To my mind, there were two categories of suspects when evaluating this untimely death: those whose motives had to do with the condo project and those whose motives had to do with the affair the man might have been conducting.

And then there was the fact that Maggie's tea had been poisoned. I'd spoken about it to my aunt, who'd informed me that she ordered her tea from a distributor on the mainland. The tea was shipped to her at the Bait and Stitch at the beginning of every month, a loose-leaf variety that was kept fresh in an airtight canister. Maggie kept the bulk of the tea at the store but had a smaller canister that she kept at home and refilled from the larger supply as needed. Finn verified that both canisters had been contaminated. In my mind the arsenic had to have been added to the tea either prior to shipment or while it was located at the Bait and Stitch. It didn't make sense that it was poisoned prior to being shipped, so it had to have been doctored by someone who had access to the back room at the Bait and Stitch. I'd considered the list of those people with access to the tea and narrowed it down to pretty much everyone on the island.

The truth of the matter was that Maggie and Marley let a variety of people use the quilting room for their book clubs, prayer groups, men's clubs, women's organizations, and on and on. Anyone could have spiked the tea. Anyone with a motive.

Which brought me to the third seemingly independent event: the upcoming election. The only common denominators I could come up with between Maggie and Keith were the island council, the condo project, and the impending election. Keith had been a member of the island council who might have been either for or against the condo development, depending on who you talked to. Maggie, a staunch opponent of the project, was the front runner in a hotly contested campaign for Gary Pixley's seat. Gary was very vocal about his opposition to the project, and if things had run their natural course, Gary wouldn't have retired until after the vote. The way things stood now, both Maggie and Francine had to win the election for the project to be rejected. Maggie was out of town due to her illness and Francine was away due to the emotional instability of Camden Bradford's mother.

So back to my hunch: It occurred to me that, in spite of the trouble he was having with the hardware store he owned, it was beyond odd that Gary would resign from the council prior to the vote. Could it be that whoever killed Keith and poisoned Maggie had managed to threaten Gary into resigning early?

Gary's hardware store was located at the edge of town. It was a nice day, so I decided to ride my bike into town. Max trotted along beside me as we made our way along the narrow dirt trail that hugged the coastline. Although it was early in the season, the surf was cooperating nicely, so there were several diehard wave junkies dressed in wet suits who had braved the cold to catch the first waves of the season.

As I peddled along the hard-packed trail, I considered the approach I would take with Gary. If he was being threatened, simply asking him about it wasn't going to net me the answers I needed. I'd have to strike up a casual conversation and then work my way into his confidence through an open window.

I parked my bike in the rack provided for just such a use and attached the leash to Max's collar. While Gary permitted our four-legged friends in the store, he required that all dogs be restrained at all times.

"Afternoon, Gary," I greeted as Max and I trotted up to the counter.

"How'd that paint you bought a few weeks ago work out?" Gary asked about the purchase I'd made to freshen the walls in my bedroom.

"The color was perfect. Thanks for suggesting it. I'll probably do the kitchen in a month or two and I'll definitely make sure to ask your opinion."

I figured that would give Gary an opening to tell me he was leaving the island sooner rather than later, if that was, in fact, the case.

Gary didn't say anything, but he did furrow his brow.

"I'm here today because I want to do something to add some cheer to Maggie's house before she returns home. I guess you heard she's in Seattle for tests."

"I wasn't aware. Have they found anything wrong with her? She seemed to be fine one minute and then sick the next."

"They found arsenic in her system."

Gary frowned. "Arsenic? Where would she have come into contact with arsenic?"

"Someone added it to that godawful tea she drinks. The tea is so bitter, I guess she didn't even notice."

"Is she going to be okay?" Gary seemed sincerely concerned.

"She should be. I sure would like to know who did that to her, however. If she'd drunk enough it could have killed her."

"I can't imagine anyone who would do such a thing."

I looked around the store. We were alone, which was fortunate. "I've been thinking about things. It seems like it might be possible someone was poisoning Maggie to keep her from winning the election."

"Why would anyone do that?"

"Someone killed Keith," I pointed out.

Gary looked away, not meeting my eyes.

"I heard you were resigning from the council early," I added. "I have to admit I was surprised, given the current political climate. Without your vote to stop the condo project, it seems clear the proposal will pass."

I could tell by the way Gary was fidgeting around that he wasn't at all comfortable with the topic.

"If something is going on, you need to tell someone. Maggie is sick and Keith is dead. The last thing we need is another casualty."

"Things are complicated," Gary returned. "I doubt you'd understand."

"Try me."

Gary looked at the floor as he appeared to be considering my suggestion. I knew the man had no reason to confide in me, but I also realized that often times, if someone wanted to share a secret, all it really took was a persistent nudge.

"The store has been struggling for a while," Gary started. "Ever since the ferry began stopping on the island it's become easier for folks to head to the mainland for a day of shopping. Several months ago I decided it was time to shut things down.

My family and I plan to move to the East Coast to be near my parents."

"Okay, but why quit early?" I asked.

"Money."

"Someone's paying you to resign from the council early?" I asked.

"Twenty-five thousand dollars," Gary verified. "Enough for us to move and get started on a new life."

"Who's paying you to resign early?" I asked. The person who was bribing Gary had to be the same person who killed Keith and poisoned Maggie.

"I don't know. I received a text a while back that outlined the proposal. The text said that as soon as I announced my resignation from the council I would receive $10,000, and when the elections were over I'd receive the other $15,000. I thought about it some, and in the end I realized how much the money would mean to my family, so I did as I was told."

"And you received the ten grand?"

"It was deposited into my bank account the day after I turned in my early resignation."

"How did the person who bribed you have your account information?" I asked. "Did you provide it to them?"

"They didn't ask. I imagine someone from the bank is in on this."

Someone from the bank. Someone like Camden Bradford. I knew he was too nice to be real.

"Gary, I realize it may mess up your deal, but you have to tell Finn about this. Maybe he can trace the text or the money transfer."

Gary sighed. "There's more. Whoever sent the text threatened my family if I didn't cooperate. It was pretty clear that if I played along I'd be rewarded by getting a bunch of cash, but if I didn't, something equally bad would happen."

I couldn't imagine being in Gary's position. It was natural to want to take care of your family, but a man was dead and justice needed to be served.

"I'm sure Finn will be discreet. No one needs to know we talked."

Gary hesitated.

"A man is dead," I reminded him.

"Yeah, okay. Let's give him a call."

It turned out that the text had been sent from a burner phone and couldn't be traced, and the routing that had been used to transfer the money into Gary's account was much too sophisticated for anyone on the island to trace. Finn was going to look into it, and promised to keep a low profile until he had some sort of proof. At this point everyone felt it best that Gary continue on the path he'd agreed to with whoever was paying him off.

When I left Gary's store I headed to the marina to see if Danny was done for the day. It occurred to me that it was time to bring in some reinforcements, and the best—only—reinforcements I could think of were Danny and Tara.

Danny and Tara were sitting on the deck of his boat when I arrived at the marina, sharing a beer while Bandit played nearby with a ball of twine someone had given him. Max wandered over to greet the kitten, who seemed thrilled to see him. Danny tossed me one of the frosty beverages, which I sipped as I revealed the purpose for my visit.

"How are we supposed to find a killer who even Finn doesn't seem able to track down?" Tara asked.

"We talk to people and hope we catch a break," I said.

"Sounds like it might be dangerous to get involved," she commented.

I looked at Danny. He shrugged. "I'm in," he agreed. "What do you want me to do?"

"We need to create a suspect list and divide it up between us. I really should get home to Romeo and I still need to see to the cats. How about we move this discussion over to my place? I'll even cook you dinner."

"Dinner sounds good." Danny stood up.

"I have my bike," I said.

"Toss it in the back of my truck and I'll drive you and Max home," Danny offered.

After letting Romeo out and seeing to the cats in the sanctuary while Tara made dinner with Danny's help, the three of us settled around my kitchen table to come up with a strategy. We began by making a list of who might benefit from Keith's death, who might benefit from Maggie's illness, and who would want Gary gone from the island. While the three things could be unrelated, we decided to work from the premise that one person or persons was responsible for everything that was going on.

There were people like Bill Powell, who were clearly on all of the lists, and people like Keith's wife, who seemed to belong on only one.

And then there were those in the gray area, such as Camden Bradford and Francine Rivers. Camden seemed to be tied in with Bill and his project, so we could rationalize that he might want Keith dead and Gary gone. He might also want

Maggie out of the running for the council. The problem was that none of us had ever seen him in the Bait and Stitch. It seemed unlikely that he could have poisoned Maggie's tea unless he was working with an accomplice.

Which brought us to Francine. She wanted the cat sanctuary gone, and creating a situation in which Maggie was too sick to care for the animals could, in a roundabout way, accomplish that. She was also Maggie's opponent in the race for the open seat on the island council. With Maggie out of the running, she'd have a good shot at winning. But Francine was very much against the condo project. There was no way she could be in on the bribing of Gary Pixley.

"It looks like everything points to Bill Powell as our primary suspect. I say we start with him and then work our way down the list."

"Start with him how?" Tara asked. "What exactly are we supposed to do?"

"I guess we can try to determine if he has an alibi," I suggested.

"He has to be Finn's number one suspect as well as ours," Tara pointed out. "I'm sure Finn has already looked into him. Maybe you should just ask him."

"Yeah, you have a point," I admitted, "although I'm not sure he'll tell me how his investigation is going even if I ask."

"We should focus on something Finn might not be able to do," Danny said.

"Like what?" Tara groaned. "He's a cop."

"Like identify the accomplice," I suggested. "Neither Camden Bradford nor Bill Powell have spent much, if any, time in the Bait and Stitch. If one or both of them is guilty they'll have needed to used an accomplice to poison Maggie's tea. We have access to the store and no one will think twice if we hang around there. It's up to us to identify who poisoned the tea."

Chapter 14

Tuesday, May 26

When I woke up the next morning Romeo was missing. Again. The cat could be a real sweetheart, but he could also be a pain in the posterior. It was Tuesday, which meant I was supposed to meet Tara for exercise class. I was also due to visit with both Mr. Parsons and Mrs. Trexler. Since yesterday had been a holiday *Cooking With Cathy* hadn't been televised as usual, but Tara had helped me to whip up a cheeseburger pie to bring to the shut-ins. I was anxious to get to the Bait and Stitch and begin snooping around, but I really did need to find my Casanova kitty before setting out for the day.

Logic would dictate that Romeo would be found courting the fair maiden Juliet. And in this case logic wasn't wrong. Both cats were lying on a chaise on Francine's back deck. It was a nice morning, unseasonably warm, with a cloudless blue sky to offset the deep blue of the nearby sea. When I first arrived on the property I didn't see Cam, but once I arrived at the deck I noticed that he was seated at a nearby outdoor table, sipping coffee and eating muffins.

"It looks like Romeo has come a-courtin' again," I commented.

"If you must know the truth, I put him up to it."

"You put him up to it?" I asked.

"I figured if he came over you'd come around. Would you like some coffee?"

Coffee sounded wonderful, though I still didn't understand the mental mechanism that both insisted that Camden Bradford was the killer *and* compelled me to join him on the deck.

"I only have a minute. I'm supposed to meet Tara in town."

"Then perhaps a quick cup."

I sat down at the table.

"So how was your dinner with Bill Powell?" I asked. I realized the moment I finished speaking that the question came out more like an accusation."

"It was fine. I take it you don't approve."

"Bill Powell and his project are creating a lot of tension on the island. There are a lot of people who wish he'd just go back where he came from."

"Maybe." Cam offered me a muffin, which I accepted. "But there are also a lot of people who are thankful that he's come up with an affordable housing option."

"How affordable are those condos going to be once the vacationers from the mainland get wind of the project and drive the prices up by flocking to the area to purchase their own little piece of paradise?"

"I'll admit that the advertised prices are only being offered to those who buy prior to construction, and that the cost for postconstruction units will be considerably higher. Still, those who buy early are getting an excellent deal and stand to make some money in the long run."

"So Bill keeps telling everyone."

Cam sat back and looked at me. He paused, as if considering his next move. "I get the feeling there's something more going on than your opposition to the condo project. Have I done something to make you mad?"

I wanted to ask him straight out if he'd killed Keith Weaver, but that seemed a little abrupt. And it did seem like Francine had been gone an awfully long time, which made me suspect his explanation of that as well. Maybe she hadn't been in the rug, but that didn't prove she was visiting his mother either.

"Have you spoken to Francine lately?" I asked.

"Are you still worried that I killed her?"

I didn't say anything.

"She'll be back this afternoon and you can see for yourself that she's alive and well."

"That's good," I answered. "Not because I thought you killed her," I added, even though I'd had that very thought. "It's just that with the special election coming up she'll need to be here."

"I heard about that," Cam responded. "It seems like awfully short notice for such an important election."

"That's exactly what I said." I smiled.

"I believe your aunt is involved as well. Will she be back soon?" Cam asked.

"The last I heard she was coming back to the island tomorrow. I should call to verify that. I hated to worry her, so I didn't mention the election. I'm a little concerned it will be too much for her."

Cam frowned. "It would be a shame if she couldn't compete. I don't live on the island, nor have I spent a large amount of time here, but from what I've heard your aunt is a favorite in the race."

"Which is probably why someone poisoned her."

"What?" Cam spat. He really seemed surprised. Maybe he wasn't in on that piece of the conspiracy.

"I thought you'd heard. The reason she's been so sick is because someone has been putting small amounts of arsenic in her tea."

"Who would do that?"

I shrugged. "Probably the same person who killed Keith Weaver and threatened Gary Pixley."

Cam sat back and stared at me. "You still think I killed Keith Weaver."

"Didn't you?"

"Of course not. Why on earth would I kill a man I barely knew?"

I leaned forward and looked Cam in the eye. "Because he changed his mind about cooperating and you were afraid the condo project would be shot down."

Cam took a deep breath. He grabbed my hand, which made me jump, but then I realized that he wasn't really holding on all that tight.

"I didn't kill Keith Weaver. I didn't kill anyone. I didn't poison your aunt and I didn't threaten Gary Pixley or anyone else. I have no motive to do so."

I opened my mouth.

"Let me remind you that I don't even really work for the bank. I certainly don't have the level of loyalty it would require to kill someone over a business deal."

"Even if the bank lost a lot of money?"

"Even then. This is a temporary gig for me. However this vote comes out, it won't affect me personally."

Cam had a point. He planned to leave in a month anyway. Maybe I'd been all wrong about him.

"If you aren't behind this then who else could it be?" I asked.

"May I ask why you even thought it was me in the first place?" Cam asked.

"Everything points to you," I insisted.

"How so?"

"First of all, Keith Weaver's body was found in a building you have access to."

"Keith Weaver was the Realtor selling the building. He had access to the building and could very well have let the killer in."

"And then there's the fact that someone deposited ten thousand dollars into Gary Pixley's bank account. Gary never provided anyone with either his account or his routing numbers, and he has no idea who deposited the money. It has to be someone with access to his banking records."

"Someone deposited ten thousand dollars into his account?"

I explained about the text from the burner phone, the bribe, and the underlying threat. I also explained how Gary's early retirement skewed the board so that both Maggie *and* Francine had to win the election in order to block the project. I could see that Cam was beginning to get an overview of the bigger picture as I spoke.

"So you think Keith's murder, your aunt's poisoning, and Gary's text are all related to the vote on the condo project?"

"What other explanation can there be?" I asked. "If you were me, you would see how it all relates back to you. Maybe not Maggie's poisoning, but if you throw in the fact that you're responsible for Francine not being here, it looks pretty damning."

"Heck, even I suspect me now that you've explained all this."

I looked at him suspiciously.

"You know I'm kidding?"

"Yeah, okay, let's say you *are* innocent. Then it has to be Bill Powell. Who else could it be?"

Cam drummed his fingers on the table as he thought about it. He seemed to be a bright man, and if he didn't do it then maybe he could help. He certainly could help with the bank piece of the puzzle— the deposit into Gary's account—and he seemed to have an in with Bill Powell as well.

"I really don't think Powell killed Weaver, but it does seem like something's going on. I'm surprised the local deputy hasn't been in to ask about the deposit."

"We just found out about it, and I believe he was planning to go into the bank today. He might have already spoken to the local employees."

Cam seemed to come to a decision. "I'll head in and see what I can find out. I'll have a chat with Bill as well. I'm afraid I can't help you with the poisoned tea."

"I thought I'd snoop around a bit when I'm in town this afternoon," I admitted.

"Sea Grotto at seven?"

I frowned as I tried to make out what sort of response was expected. Was he asking me on a date?

"To compare notes," Cam clarified.

"I really need to get back to see to the cats, but if you want to meet you can come by my place at seven. Bring a pizza. I like pepperoni."

"Pizza it is."

After I finished my coffee I headed home to see to the cats and then get ready to go into town. My first stop was the community center for exercise class, and then I planned to work on the progressively complicated investigation I'd been drawn into. My goal for the day was to narrow down the list of people who could have poisoned Maggie's tea. A lot of people had access to the tea, but I was willing to bet there weren't a lot of people who had a motive to make Maggie sick. Marley was at the store every day from opening to close. Maybe she'd noticed someone lingering in the back room. I figured I'd speak to her first, and if she didn't have any insight I'd make a list of all the groups that used the store after-hours.

I said good-bye to Tara after class, considering heading straight over to the Bait and Stitch, but Tuesday was my regular day to visit with both Mr. Parsons and Mrs. Trexler and I didn't want to disappoint either of them by not showing up. I headed to Mr. Parsons first because his residence was the closest.

"Mr. Parsons, it's Cait," I called into the intercom that was located at the front door. The door clicked open and I made my way inside. I was happy to see that the house was still tidy.

I peeked into the study expecting to see Mr. Parsons alone, but instead I found him sitting at the chess table with Cody.

"You remember Cody," Mr. Parsons introduced.

"I do," I answered. It annoyed me that the man kept showing up when I was trying so hard to forget him and get on with my life. "I just stopped by to drop off a casserole and see if you needed anything from the store."

"Cody was nice enough to bring me some groceries, but the casserole sounds good. You can put it in the refrigerator and then come back for a visit."

"I wouldn't want to interrupt your game. Besides, I have a lot to get done today."

"Very well. Thanks for coming by." Mr. Parsons returned his attention to the game. Even Rambler, who was lying at Cody's feet, neglected to say hi. I can't remember the last time I felt so underappreciated.

I put the casserole in the refrigerator before heading to Mrs. Trexler's home, which was in Pelican Bay, near the harbor. At least she'd be glad to see me. As far as I knew, Cody had never established a relationship with her, like he had with Mr. Parsons.

"Mrs. Trexler," I called as I knocked on the front door. I listened, waiting for her to answer. I always become concerned when one of the seniors I visited don't answer right away. Anything could happen, and there comes a point when it's unwise to continue to live alone.

"Mrs. Trexler, it's Caitlin Hart," I called again.

I tried the front door, but it was locked. I walked around the house and looked in through the windows but couldn't see anything out of the ordinary. I tried the back door, which was likewise locked. I was about to call Finn to ask him to come out when the neighbor next door peeked over the back fence.

"Susan isn't home," the woman informed me.

I frowned. "I was just here on Friday and she didn't mention going anywhere. Do you know where she went?" I asked the woman.

"No. She didn't say a thing."

"When did you say she left?" I wondered.

"This morning. Early. Around five thirty."

I didn't like the sound of a last-minute trip so early in the morning, but there wasn't anything I could do about it. I said good-bye and headed to the Bait and Stitch to speak to Marley about possible suspects in Maggie's poisoning. It seemed the town was being inundated with mysterious occurrences, but the one I cared most about solving related to my aunt and her illness.

"I can't think of a single person who would want to make Maggie sick," Marley insisted when I broached the subject. Luckily, the weekend crowds had gone, leaving the store empty at this time of day.

"Maggie is great," I agreed, "and we both love her. But she can be outspoken and she has on occasion rubbed people the wrong way. We need to narrow things down a bit and decide who had access to the tea *and* might have wanted her out of the way."

Marley frowned as she thought about it. While Maggie and Marley were both in their late sixties, Marley had more of a grandmother vibe going on, while Maggie was more of a wild and crazy aunt. Marley wore her graying hair in a long braid, while Maggie kept her blond hair short and stylishly highlighted. Marley was soft and mommish, while Maggie was fit and athletic. Or at least she had been until she got sick. Now . . . well, now she looked pale, thin, and frail.

"Berta Perkins did say she was put out when Maggie refused to support her campaign to have part of the funding for the library diverted to the arts program," Marley finally said.

Berta owned an art gallery that sold high-end products, but she was also involved in a local arts program that held classes at the high school a couple of nights a week. Funding for the program had been cut, and Berta had argued that the money remaining in the island's discretionary account, which covered the library as well as the theater arts program, should be divided equally. Maggie had come out in support of sharing the money between the theater arts and the arts programs but was steadfastly against using any of the library funds, arguing that the library provided a service to a larger percentage of the island's population.

"And her group has been using the Bait and Stitch on Wednesday evenings for the needlework group she's been involved with," Marley added.

I wasn't certain that being upset over support for a funding issue was a good motive for poisoning someone, but Berta did have a motive and she had opportunity, so I added her to the list.

"Okay," I said, "who else?"

Marley thought about it. "Well, Francine Rivers, of course. She's not only angry with your aunt over the cat sanctuary but she's also Maggie's opponent in the council race. Maggie is the front runner, but Francine has a really good chance if Maggie had to drop out. And she's here for both the Thursday book club and the senior women's group on Mondays."

I'd already thought of Francine, but I hated to think she'd stoop so low. The two women had been friends for a lot of years until the cats came between them. Still, she did have opportunity and motive, so I wrote her name down.

"Speaking of the senior women's group, I spoke to Patience Tillman the other day, and she mentioned that the group planned to support Francine in the election. It was my understanding that they were going to back Maggie. Do you know why they changed their minds?"

"Apparently, Patience is convinced that her husband, Toby, has eyes for Maggie."

I frowned. "Why would she think that? Maggie surely hasn't . . ."

"Maggie didn't do anything, but Toby does tend to spend a lot of time hanging around the store when Maggie's here. Even more so since she's been sick. He claims he needs to buy fishing supplies, but he seems to draw each visit out and goes out of his way to do little things for Maggie that she's too weak to do herself. Some might say he's just being neighborly, but I can see why Patience feels the way she does."

"Jealousy is a strong motive for violence," I said.

I added Patience to the list, which, I had to admit, was pretty weak. While all of these women might have motive and opportunity, I was certain none of them would actually put arsenic in Maggie's tea.

"Is there anyone else?" I asked hopefully. "Anyone at all? Maybe someone who's been lurking around more often than they normally do?"

"Maggie's tea is delivered once a month," Marley pointed out. "Whoever is tampering with it doesn't necessarily need to be hanging around a lot. They only need to be here when the new tea arrives."

Marley was right. I was never going to figure this out with my current line of reasoning.

Not only had I not solved the mystery I'd set out to wrap up that day but I had a new one to add to my ever-growing list. I'd asked Finn about looking into Mrs.

Trexler's disappearance, but he'd insisted it seemed she'd left of her own free will. I decided I'd check the next day, and if she still wasn't back . . . well, I didn't know what I'd do.

By the time Cam showed up at my door with the pizza I was starving. I realized I hadn't taken the time to eat since the early morning coffee I'd shared with the man who was creating quite a lot of confusion in my mind and my emotions. After we'd helped ourselves to several pieces each, we retired to the front deck to watch the sun set.

"So did you have any luck?" I asked as I sipped the excellent wine Cam had brought.

"It took a lot longer than I planned, but I managed to do some backtracking. The money that was deposited into Gary Pixley's account originated from the Cayman Islands. The account that paid it out belongs to a company that I now know is associated with Bill Powell's overseas operations."

"So Bill did it. I knew it! The guy is a snake."

"Actually, we don't know that Bill did anything. He's claiming he had no knowledge of the transfer, and there are a handful of people who work for him who could have initiated the payoff, including his CFO and his operations manager, who's based on the island where the bank transfer occurred."

"Maybe one of these men transferred the money, but neither of them is on this island, so they couldn't have killed Keith Weaver or poisoned my aunt. It has to be Bill," I insisted.

Cam took a sip from his own wineglass. "I know you'd like to see this wrapped up, but keep in mind that we still don't know if the three incidents are related. I do think it's unlikely that one of Bill's employees would have initiated the payoff to Gary Pixley without Bill's consent. Deputy Finnegan thinks so as well and has brought him in for questioning. Hopefully, we'll know more by tomorrow. In the meantime, we have a forensic accountant looking at all of Bill's financial dealings."

Romeo got up from his napping spot on the swing and jumped into Cam's lap.

"He seems to really like you," I commented as the cat began to purr.

"He's a great cat." Cam began scratching him behind the ears. "I'm a bit worried about him now that Francine is back."

"Worried?" I asked.

"I'm pretty sure she realized her Juliet had been defiled, and I'm equally sure she knows who the Casanova is who defiled her. I'm surprised she hasn't already been by to read you the riot act."

"Great. Something to look forward to. Did she say how your mom is doing?"

"Better. I guess I'll see myself when I get back to the mainland. I missed the last ferry tonight and Wednesdays are my regular day at the bank, but I should head back tomorrow evening."

"Are you staying with Francine for the night?" I asked.

"I thought I'd check into the bed and breakfast in town."

"You can sleep on my sofa," I found myself offering. What? Was I stupid? Less than twenty-four hours ago I thought the man was a killer and now I was offering him a spot on my sofa?

Cam smiled. "It sounds like an offer that might be worth accepting."

"I'm only offering the sofa. Nothing more," I emphasized. "Besides, if Francine does come by to defend Juliet's honor, you'll be here to help defend Romeo."

"Okay, I accept, then."

"I need to head over to see to the cats in the sanctuary. Would you like to come along?"

"Yeah, I'd like that. I've been curious about the cause of the tantrum Francine seems to throw every time the sanctuary is brought up. How many cats do you exactly have?"

I filled Cam in on the demographic makeup of our current residents as we walked across the lawn toward the large wooden building. "I expect our population to grow any day now because we have two cats about to deliver. Luckily, I also have two litters that are ready for homes, so things will even themselves out."

Several of the cats trotted over to greet us when we walked into the building. Even the most antisocial cat knew that when Maggie or I appeared, food was on its way, so most showed interest in my arrival. I gave Cam the grand tour, cleaning litter boxes and filling food and water bowls as I made my way from cat room to cat room.

"The cats in this room are the ones that have been fully socialized," I informed Cam as we entered the last of them. "They're ready for adoption as soon as we can find them forever homes."

"And how do you do that?" Cam seemed interested.

"Currently, Maggie or I take the cats to adoption clinics once or twice a month on the mainland. Once Coffee Cat Books is opened we plan to spotlight four or five at a time in the cat lounge. We hope the cats and their prospective owners will find each other."

"Speaking of Coffee Cat Books," Cam began, "I meant to tell you that I received final approval for your loan as I was walking out the door."

"Really?" I screeched with happiness.

"The final paperwork should be available to sign tomorrow."

"Thank you." I hugged Cam. He seemed surprised and then hugged me back.

I took a step back. "Tara will be so happy. I should call her."

"Go ahead. I'll finish up in here and then meet you back at the house. It's the least I can do for letting me stay with you tonight."

"Are you sure?" I hesitated.

"Don't worry. I can clean a couple of cat boxes and refill food and water dishes."

I hugged Cam again. "Thanks. Just pull the door closed when you're done. It locks automatically."

Chapter 15

Wednesday, May 27

The next morning I heard a knocking on the door just as I was about to get into the shower. It was probably Francine, here to read me the riot act about Romeo's potential bastard children.

"Can you get that?" I called to Cam, who I'd left at the kitchen table drinking coffee.

I heard voices in the background as I stuck my head under the warm spray, so I assumed he'd done as I'd asked. My invitation to Cam had been spontaneous the previous evening, but it turned out that we'd had a nice evening. As expected, Tara was over-the-moon happy when I informed her that we'd been approved for the full amount of our loan and insisted on coming over so we could discuss the remodel, which she was itching to get started. Cam, Tara, and I had talked late into the evening. The fruit of our conversation was a plan that was far superior to what Tara and I had come up with on our own. There was no doubt about it; Cam was a savvy businessman who knew what he was doing. No wonder he'd made so much money in what couldn't have been all that long a career.

I tried to figure out how old Cam was. It seemed rude to come right out and ask, but I found that I was curious. He'd mentioned that he had an MBA, which I figured must have taken two years or so to complete. If he'd graduated high school when he was eighteen, that would have made him twenty-four when he graduated college and grad school.

He'd mentioned that he'd worked in banking for ten years before deciding he'd had enough. That would bring him up to thirty-four. I seemed to remember him saying that he'd been traveling the world for the past couple of years, so I imagined Cam was thirty-six or thirty-seven. He'd also talked about wanting to find a new career when he'd completed the job he'd agreed to do for his brother. It seemed to me that it would be difficult to start all over again at this point in his life, but maybe that was just because from where I stood, thirty-seven sounded too old to learn new tricks.

When I returned to the kitchen it was empty. Cam had said he needed to leave for work. Francine hadn't lingered, and Romeo seemed to be fine, so I imagined

Cam had handled the feisty woman without bloodshed. I still had a strange feeling about the banker, but I had to admit I was going to miss having him living next door. Romeo was going to miss him as well. It seemed that my vagabond cat had really bonded with the guy.

After seeing to the cats I headed into town and the Bait and Stitch. Maggie had called to say that she was going to be coming home on the Thursday morning ferry, and I wanted to be sure that everything was in tip-top shape when she arrived.

"You spent the night with Camden Bradford?" Danny accused seconds after he walked through the front door of the Bait and Stitch.

"I so did not," I defended. "Well, actually, I did. But it's not what you think."

By this point Marley and the women at the quilting table had 100 percent of their attention focused on Danny and me.

"He was at your cabin at seven-thirty this morning."

"He slept on the sofa. Francine is back and he was due to work at the island branch today. Besides, he missed the last ferry."

"If he's friends with Francine he could have stayed with her," Danny pointed out.

"Or you could have let him stay at Maggie's," Marley added.

I glared at both of them. "Who I allow to sleep on my sofa is my business."

Marley looked away, but Danny opened his mouth as if to speak.

"You're my brother, not my father," I added for good measure.

Someone at the table behind me snickered.

"Besides, how do you even know that Cam spent the night at the cabin?" I asked.

"Cody told me," Danny said.

"Cody? How in the heck does Cody know who I did or did not spend the night with?"

"He stopped by this morning to speak to you and Camden Bradford answered the door. He told Cody you were in the shower."

"Oh, my," one of the women sitting at the table giggled.

Great. News of my overnight guest would probably make the front page of the island's newspaper. If we still had an island paper, that is.

"That's because I *was* in the shower," I explained. "I heard someone knock on the door, but I thought it was Francine, come to read me the riot act for allowing Romeo to defile her Juliet."

I rolled my eyes. *All* the women at the quilting table were snickering now.

"I don't think it's a good idea to let strange men sleep at your place, even if they are sleeping on the sofa," Danny warned.

"And I don't think it's a good idea to take strange women back to your boat when you can't even remember their names," I shot back.

Suddenly half of the women in the room gasped.

Danny looked over my shoulder. "Perhaps this is a conversation best left for another time."

"Yeah," I had to agree. It was.

"The main reason I ran into Cody in the first place was because I went to talk to Finn and Cody was there."

I frowned. "Why was Cody at Finn's?"

"They were friends," Danny reminded me. "Actually, they still are."

I guess that was true. Damn small-town living.

"So why did you go to see Finn?" I asked.

"I wanted to see how he was doing on the case."

"Camden didn't kill anyone," I asserted. I know I've been the number one spokesperson for his guilt, but somewhere along the line I guess I'd accepted he was innocent.

"Yeah, that's Finn's conclusion as well."

"So if Finn has come to the conclusion that Cam is innocent, did he say why?" I asked.

"He's been working to follow the money deposited into Gary Pixley's account and found a document with Bill Powell's signature."

"I knew it," I trumpeted.

"It was a forgery. Camden Bradford offered the proof."

Okay, I was somewhat deflated. "So what does that prove?" I asked. "If they're working together like we thought, he could just be covering for him."

"You still aren't sure he's innocent," Danny charged.

I blushed.

"There's a part of you that still believes he's a killer and you let him stay at your place. How dumb are you?"

"Pretty dumb, I guess. So what proof did Cam offer that led Finn to believe he's innocent?"

"I guess the *B* in Bill's name was very distinct, so he was able to identify the person who forged the signature as his brother-in-law."

Everyone, including me, gasped.

"Finn said Cam was really torn up when he found out that his brother-in-law was in on the blackmail from the beginning. Finn seems to think he gave up a lot to turn him in."

"Poor Cam. He gave up six months of his life for his brother-in-law and the guy was involved in dirty dealing all the while. Did his sister know?"

"He wasn't sure. He didn't think so, but he was on his way to find out when I left."

So Cam's brother-in-law—in an effort to further his own career, I imagine—made a deal with someone from Bill Powell's company.

"Was Bill in on it?" I asked.

"Finn doesn't think so. Why allow someone to forge your signature if you're in on it? He was planning to have a discussion with Bill in an attempt to get to the bottom of things."

"Does Finn think the men behind the blackmail were responsible for Keith Weaver's death?" I wondered.

"It looks that way," Danny said.

"And Maggie's poisoning?"

"I don't see how those men could be responsible for that."

"I was afraid of that."

Chapter 16

St. Patrick's is a very traditional Catholic church. Most consider it to be the cornerstone of the village of Harthaven. It's a large brick building with two wings and a bell tower. Father Kilian lives in a smaller house that adjoins the church and is famous for his beautifully maintained flower garden. On the opposite side of the large piece of land which the church shares with the cemetery is an even smaller house that's occupied by Sister Mary, the only nun assigned to the island. While Father Kilian sees to the needs of the congregation as a whole, Sister Mary focuses on the children's program.

When I arrived at practice as promised, I was warmly greeted by the children who sang in the choir, as well as many of the parents who stayed behind to watch. I'd been a member of the choir when I was a child and had helped out from time to time since I'd moved on to the adult choir, so I knew most of those involved with the group. I have to admit I was beginning to feel a sense of excitement about the obligation my mother had talked me into.

"Where is Mrs. Cleary?" I asked. Mrs. Cleary had been accompanying the children's choir on the piano since I'd been a member of the group.

"She had to go to her daughter's," a cute girl with brown ringlets answered. "She had a baby. Mrs. Darby is going to fill in."

"Thank you," I said, hesitating as I tried to remember the girl's name. "Stella? Right?"

"Yes, ma'am."

"You can call me Cait."

"No, ma'am. Mama wouldn't like it."

"Okay, then, how about Ms. Cait?"

"That should be fine." The girl smiled.

"I hope Mrs. Darby remembers she's supposed to fill in tonight. She's already fifteen minutes late." After everything that had been going on with Keith Weaver, I supposed it wouldn't be unheard of for Kim to forget her obligation.

"Her car wouldn't start so Mr. Cody went to get her," Stella informed me.

"Mr. Cody?" I felt my enthusiasm ebb just a bit.

"Yes, ma'am. He's going to help you with us. My mama said he's a real American hero and a cherished member of the community. She wanted to be sure we all were polite and did our best for him."

"I see. Well, I guess we should go ahead and get started with the introductions. Maybe Mr. Cody and Mrs. Darby will be here by the time we're finished." I looked toward the larger group, whose members were mingling around the room. "Okay, let's all line up in your usual positions," I announced in the loudest voice I could muster.

By the time Cody had returned with Kim, the introductions had been completed and we transitioned directly into the music, leaving no opportunity for me to chat with either Cody or Kim. If I had to guess I'd say this hadn't been the first time Cody had helped out. The kids seemed to know and like him, and he had no problem singing along with the group as they rehearsed the songs for the Founders Day pageant.

By the time the rehearsal was over, I was both drained and energized. The children had beautiful voices, and unlike the group who performed when I was a child, they all seemed polite and well behaved. I tried to take a moment to speak with each parent when they picked up their child. By the time the last child had left, it was well in to the evening. My grumbling stomach reminded me that I hadn't eaten since that morning.

"Did Cody leave?" I asked Kim, who was sitting at the piano, playing a soft melody.

"He's over at the house, talking to Father Kilian. I hope he won't be too long. I'm exhausted and would really like to get home."

"I can drive you," I offered. "It's on my way and I'm ready to leave."

"Thanks." Kim shut the lid to the piano. "I'd appreciate that. I'll just text Cody to let him know I have a ride so he can visit for as long as he likes."

Kim and I turned off all the lights and made sure everything was locked up before we headed out to the parking lot and my clunker of a car. It was cloudy that evening, with a hint of rain in the air. We'd actually just come through a dry spell, so a little rain would be nice. I did hope that it would hold off until I returned home, though; my windshield wipers really needed to be replaced.

"So did you hear that they might have found Keith's killer?" I asked once I pulled away from the church parking lot.

"They have?" Kim sounded surprised. "I didn't think they even had any suspects."

"They really didn't, but it turned out that some forgeries were discovered at the bank, and the sheriff thinks they might be connected to Keith's murder. As far as I know, they haven't made an arrest yet, but if you ask me, it's just a matter of time until they do."

I glanced at Kim out of the corner of my eye. She had a huge smile on her face. I guess I could see why she would be happy that Keith's killer might have been caught, but the size of her grin and the fact that she didn't even ask who the suspected killer was seemed odd.

"I guess the man who forged the papers must be the same man Keith made a deal with prior to his death," I fished.

"I guess he must be."

"What I don't understand is why Keith would make a deal with this guy in the first place. Unlike the other person involved, Keith didn't appear to need money." I decided it was best at that point not to mention Gary's name.

"No," Kim confirmed. "He had plenty of money."

"I suppose he must have been after something else."

Kim shrugged.

"Or maybe he was being blackmailed," I offered. "There's been a rumor going around about him having an affair."

Kim frowned. "You think Keith was being blackmailed?"

"I don't really know, but it seems plausible." I turned onto Kim's street. "I suppose if he was being blackmailed, the blackmailer must know who Keith was having the affair with. I imagine it will all come out once Finn gets him to talk."

"Who is this person the police suspect of the blackmail?" Kim asked.

"I really shouldn't say."

Kim reached for the door handle as I pulled up to the curb. "But you know who it is?"

"Yes," I confirmed.

"Would you like to come in?" Kim asked.

I hesitated. I hated to be rude, but I really did want to get home. "I should get back so I can see to the cats."

"Just for a minute," Kim persuaded. "It looks like the house is dark. Kourtney is out and my husband is away. I'd appreciate someone coming inside with me while I turn on the lights. I've been a little spooked since Keith's death."

I turned off the ignition. "Okay, but just for a minute. I really do need to get home."

I followed Kim up the walkway as the first clap of thunder vibrated through the night sky. Kim used her key to unlock the door as the first drops of rain began to hit the pavement. I followed her inside as she made her way across the dark room and flipped on a light. I waited by the entry while she turned on lights farther down the hall. My eyes were drawn to airline tickets lying on a table near the entry. I'm not sure why I did it, but I picked them up and looked at them. There were two tickets to Rio that had been torn in half. My hand began to shake as I realized that one of the tickets was in her name and the other was in Keith's.

"Nosy much?" Kim asked when she walked back into the room.

I looked at Kim and suddenly I knew. She was the woman Keith had been having the affair with. Cassie had said that Kourtney's dad had left her mom because of some big fight. Could the fight have been over Keith Weaver?

"You're the woman Keith was having the affair with," I unwisely said.

"It wasn't an affair. We were in love. We planned to run away together."

I looked at the tickets, which confirmed two first-class seats for flight 630 out of Seattle.

"But he changed his mind," I realized.

"The bastard told me he had a change of heart *after* my husband left me and my marriage was destroyed. What kind of a monster does a thing like that?"

"Someone found out about the affair and he was being blackmailed," I realized. "That's why he was going to change his vote."

Kim continued to stare at me, but she didn't respond.

"But at the last minute he had a change of heart," I decided.

"It was just a stupid project and he was willing to throw away everything we had in order to block the development. Not only did he have the audacity to suggest that he regretted his decision to vote in favor of Bill Powell's project but he also regretted his decision to leave his wife. After everything I gave up for him, he was going to work things out with her."

"So you killed him."

"I didn't mean to. We went to the cannery to take some measurements for the newspaper ad Keith planned to run. We got to talking, and he told me that he'd had a change of heart about both the vote and leaving his wife. I totally lost it. We started arguing and I picked up a board and hit him over the head."

"You have to tell Finn what happened," I instructed. "It will go easier for you if you turn yourself in."

"I'm not going to turn myself in," Kim said firmly.

"But . . ." I'd just started to argue when I saw her reach into her purse and pull out a small gun.

"You have a gun," I said lamely.

"I've lived with a violent man for the past twenty years." Kim looked at the weapon in her hand. "I always thought it would be him that I'd one day use it on. Funny how life works out."

"You're going to shoot me?" I screeched.

"You've left me no choice."

"You know, people say that, but in most cases, such as this one, it really isn't true," I pointed out. "You have a lot of choices." I inched toward the door. "Good choices."

"Like what?" Kim raised the gun and pointed it at my chest.

"You could let me go."

"And why would I do that? You'd run to Finn and I'd never get away in time."

"The tickets have been destroyed," I said.

"I can have them replaced. Besides, I only need one."

"But Kourtney . . ." I reminded her of her daughter.

"She wants to live with her loser of a father and I've decided to let her. She's with him now. I lied before. I guess I could just tie you up until I land in Rio and then call and let someone know where you are."

"But the flight is in two days' time," I pointed out.

"Would you rather I shoot you?" Kim asked.

"No. Your plan makes sense."

I decided to cooperate while Kim led me to her basement and locked the door. At least she didn't bother to tie me up. Not that I was going anywhere. The windowless room was dark and dank, and I could only image what was slithering around on the dirt floor. I sat down on the floor near the door and prayed that someone human would find me before someone reptile did.

Chapter 17

Thursday, May 28

I had no concept of how long I'd been in the basement or what time it was. I heard voices overhead, followed by a shot and then multiple footsteps. I closed my eyes against the light as someone opened the basement door.

"Cait, are you in here?" I recognized Cody's voice.

"Is she in there?" I heard Danny ask.

"I'm here," I called from the back of the dark room.

My eyes refused to adjust to the light, so I couldn't see who picked me up and carried me up the stairs, but I could tell by his scent that it was Cody.

"How long have I been down there?" I asked.

"It's Thursday morning. Late morning," Danny specified. "I came by your place to pick you up so we could meet Maggie's ferry, but you weren't home. It was obvious you hadn't been home. Max hadn't been let out and the cats hadn't been seen to. I knew you had choir practice last night, so I called Cody, who told me you'd left there with Kim. I called Finn, who'd already suspected Kim was the killer."

"The shot?" I asked as I continued to keep my eyes closed.

"Kim," Cody answered. "She shot at us but missed. Finn has her in custody. We should get you to the hospital."

"I don't need to go to the hospital. I'm fine. My eyes just need to adjust to the light."

I tried to open my eyes, but it was going to take a while for my day vision to recover.

"What about Maggie?" I asked.

"Tara went to pick her up. I imagine they're at the house by now."

I leaned my head against Cody's strong chest and listened to the steady rhythm of his heart. It felt safe and comforting. I let the tension leave my body as I relaxed in his arms.

"Let's go home," I suggested.

Cody carried me out to the car. I could hear Danny and Finn talking. Finn agreed to come by the house to talk to me after he wrapped everything up with Kim. Danny must have driven, because Cody continued to hold me until he placed me safely on my own sofa with a frantic Max looking out for me.

Danny brought me a pair of sunglasses, which allowed my eyes to slowly adjust to the light. It felt good to be home among family and friends. To be honest, there were times during my long stay in Kim's basement when I'd doubted I ever would be again.

"I really enjoyed spending time with Siobhan, but I'm so happy to be home." Maggie helped herself to a second serving of the casserole Tara had brought by. "I missed everyone so much."

We were all glad to have Maggie home as well, especially Akasha, who hadn't left her side.

"I still can't believe Kim killed Keith and tried to kill you," Maggie said to me.

"I think killing Keith was an accident, an act of rage she later regretted. And I don't think she planned to kill me. She just wanted me detained until she could follow through with her plan to leave the country," I answered.

"I do feel bad for her," Marley commented.

"She was a married woman fooling around with a married man," Maggie countered. "She brought her problems on herself. It's poor Mr. Bradford I feel bad for. Have you heard whether they've determined if his sister was involved?" Maggie looked at Finn, who'd decided to stay after coming by to talk to me about Kim.

"It appears Camden Bradford's sister knew nothing about the blackmail of Keith Weaver or the bribery of Gary Pixley. When Bill Powell first brought the project to the attention of the bank he was looking for private investors to get the developmental stages off the ground. His site foreman, as well as Bradford's brother-in-law, each invested a significant amount of money. When it looked like the project might be blocked by the council they panicked. They blackmailed Keith and bribed Gary in order to ensure that the proposal passed."

"And we're sure these men aren't responsible for poisoning Maggie's tea?" I asked.

"It doesn't look like it," Finn confirmed. "As odd as it might seem, it appears we had three separate things going on that just seemed to be related on the surface."

"Don't worry." Danny squeezed my hand. "We'll get whoever was responsible for making Maggie sick. Cody and I have been working on a plan."

"Is that right?" I looked at Cody.

"Hey, I helped as well," Tara chimed in.

"I agree to take a nap and miss all the fun," I joked.

Max barked as the doorbell rang.

"I'll get it," I offered.

I couldn't imagine who would be stopping by at this time of the evening. It turned out to be Francine, with Romeo in her arms.

"I'm so sorry," I blurted as I opened the door.

"May I speak with you for a moment?" Francine asked.

"Sure, come on in. We're having dinner. Would you like to join us?"

"No. I can only stay a moment. I want to talk to you about Romeo."

"I've tried to keep him inside. I really have," I assured her. "He's a tricky cat who's way too smart for his own good."

"Yes, well, it seems Juliet is quite taken with him. Until he moved in with you, she was content to stay inside, but now I find her sneaking out on a regular basis."

"I'm so sorry. I'll find him another home."

"That's what I wanted to ask you about. If it's okay with you, I'd like to take him."

I couldn't have been more surprised if Francine had dumped a bucket of ice water over my head.

"You want him to live with you?"

"I'm afraid Juliet will just continue to sneak out otherwise. I have a feeling if we allow them to be together both cats will stay put. I suspect it might be too late to defend Juliet's virtue at this point anyway. It's early to tell for sure, but I suspect kittens are on the way, and it only seems right that they have a mother and a father to watch out for them."

I smiled.

"You, of course, can visit with Romeo any time you want." Francine took a deep breath. "Do we have a deal?"

I hugged the tiny woman. "We have a deal."

Recipes by Kathi

Orange Muffins
Beefiladas
Irish Stew
Brandied Cherry Cheesecake

Contributed by Readers

Cedar Planked Salmon – contributed by Vivian Shane
Cheeseburger Pie – contributed by Connie Correll
Johnny Marzetti Casserole – contributed by Joyce Aiken
Cottage Pudding – contributed by Melissa Nicholson

Feline Recipe
Kitty Pretzel – contributed by Robin Coxon

Orange Muffins

Ingredients:

1½ cups vegetable oil
3 eggs
1¼ cups milk
2¼ cups sugar
¼ cup orange juice
3 tsp. orange extract
3 cups flour
1½ tsp. salt
1½ tsp. baking powder

Preheat oven to 350 degrees. In a large mixing bowl, beat oil, eggs, milk, sugar, orange juice, and orange extract until smooth. Add in flour, salt, and baking powder and mix.

Line cupcake pan with cupcake liners (makes 24).

Bake at 350 degrees for 25 minutes, or until toothpick comes out clean.

Cream Frosting:

8 oz. cream cheese, softened
2½ cups powdered sugar
1 tsp. orange extract
½ cup heavy whipping cream

Mix cream cheese, powdered sugar, orange extract, and heavy whipping cream in small bowl. Beat until smooth.

Frost the tops of each cooled muffin.

Beefiladas

Ingredients:
2 lbs. boneless rib roast
Seasoned salt, garlic powder, pepper
40 oz. salsa (approx.) (I use half hot and half mild)

8 oz. diced green chilies
1 cup sour cream
8 flour tortillas
2–3 cups grated cheddar cheese

Trim all fat off boneless rib roast. Season with salt, pepper, and garlic powder. Place in slow cooker. Cover meat with store-bought salsa, either hot or mild, depending on preference.

Cook on high until meat begins to pull apart. Continue to shred meat as it cooks. When it's completely done (cooking time depends on size of meat and heat of slow cooker, but about 8 hours), spoon meat from sauce with slotted spoon. Reserve sauce.

Mix meat in a large bowl with diced green chilies and sour cream.

Place ⅛ of meat mixture in a taco-size flour tortilla. Place in a large greased baking pan (9 x 13).

Cover meat with reserved sauce *or* cover meat with canned enchilada sauce; in my family there's a division as to which is preferable, so experiment a bit.

Cover with grated cheddar cheese. Bake at 350° for 45 minutes.

Irish Stew

Ingredients:
1 tbs. olive oil
1 lb. beef stew meat
2 cloves garlic, minced
1 onion, chopped
4 large carrots, peeled and chopped
¼ tsp. dried thyme
½ tsp. dried parsley
2 cups beef broth
2 tbs. butter, melted
2 tbs. all-purpose flour
1 tsp. salt
1 tsp. pepper

Mashed potatoes:
4 baking potatoes, peeled and chopped into large chunks
6 tbs. butter
4 cloves garlic, smashed
3 tbs. milk

Brown the meat in olive oil. Add garlic, onion, carrots, and spices. Cook for 5 minutes before adding beef broth. Cover and simmer over medium-low heat for at least 2 hours.

After about 1½ hours, make mashed potatoes.

Boil potatoes for about 20 minutes or until fork tender. Drain potatoes and mash with the butter, garlic, and milk.

Mix the melted butter and flour together. Add slowly to the stew.

Continue to cook for 10 more minutes.

Serve the stew over the mashed potatoes.

Brandied Cherry Cheesecake

Crust:
1¾ cups graham cracker crumbs
⅓ cup butter or margarine, melted

Filling:
4 packages (8 oz. each) cream cheese, softened
1½ cups granulated sugar
⅓ cup whipping cream
1 tbs. vanilla
3 eggs

Sauce:
¼ cup butter or margarine
½ cup packed brown sugar
½ cup brandy
1 can cherry pie filling
1 tbs. cornstarch

Heat oven to 350°. In small bowl, mix crust ingredients. Press firmly in bottom of greased 2-qt. baking pan. Bake 10 minutes. Cool completely. Reduce oven temperature to 325°.

While crust is cooling, in large bowl, beat all filling ingredients except eggs with electric mixer on medium speed about 1 minute or until smooth. On low speed, beat in eggs until well blended. Pour over crust; smooth top.

Bake 90 minutes or until set.

Refrigerate until chilled.

In saucepan, melt butter. Mix in brown sugar and brandy. Heat to boiling over medium heat, stirring constantly. Stir in pie filling and heat to boiling. Add cornstarch. Boil 3 to 4 minutes, stirring constantly, until slightly thickened. Let cool slightly and then pour over cheesecake.
Refrigerate.

Cedar Planked Salmon

Contributed by Vivian Shane

I live in the Pacific Northwest, where salmon is a staple, and I am so fortunate that I have a fisherman neighbor who shares his catch quite frequently. This recipe is my favorite way to prepare it. Just add some fresh corn from the farmers market and a great wine from your favorite vineyard—a perfect summer evening meal! A bonus is that the cedar plank really smells great while the fish is cooking.

Soak a cedar plank in water for 4 hours (my grocery store carries the planks at the meat/fish counter). Season the salmon (see dry rub recipe below) and place, skin-side down, on the soaked plank. Place plank on grill using low/medium heat. Close lid and grill fish for 10–20 minutes or until fish flakes easily; there's no need to turn the fish. The plank will smoke lightly, creating a cedar aroma. Avoid unnecessarily opening the grill lid to prevent loss of heat and smoke. Use a spray bottle to put out any flare-ups. Allow the plank to cool before discarding.

Dry Rub:
1½ tbs. salt
2 tbs. brown sugar
1 tbs. black pepper
1 tbs. garlic powder
1 tbs. dried basil
1 tbs. paprika

Cheeseburger Pie

Contributed by Connie Correll

My sons always piled into this, so I used 3 pounds of hamburger and doubled the remaining ingredients, using a cake pan to bake it in!

Ingredients:

1 lb. ground beef
1 cup (or to taste) chopped onion
½ tsp. salt (can omit for certain diets)
1 cup milk
½ cup Bisquick baking mix
2 eggs
1 cup shredded cheddar cheese

Cook ground beef and onion; drain. Stir in salt. Spread in a 9-inch pie plate. Mix together milk, Bisquick, and eggs until blended. Pour over meat. Bake 15 minutes at 400°, then sprinkle cheese on top and bake an additional 10 minutes.

There could be variations to this by adding taco seasoning to the burger, or even replacing the burger with diced ham and using Swiss cheese for a breakfast idea!

Johnny Marzetti Casserole

Contributed by Joyce Aiken

I tasted this at a church potluck about thirty years ago and really liked it. The woman who brought it was a good cook; she has since passed away. I guess I should have asked her who Johnny Marzetti was and why she named the casserole after him!

2 lbs. ground beef
I onion, chopped
⅔ cup green pepper, chopped
2 cups fresh mushrooms, sliced
½ tsp. pepper
Salt to taste
1 tsp. oregano
2 tbs. Worcestershire sauce
2 cups tomato sauce
8 oz. egg noodles
8 oz. shredded cheddar cheese

Brown meat. Add onions, green pepper, mushrooms, and seasonings. Cook until veggies are tender. Add Worcestershire and tomato sauces. Simmer gently while you cook the noodles as per package directions in a separate pot.

Spray a 9 x 13–inch pan with PAM. Spread half of noodles, half of meat mixture, and half of cheese. Repeat layers.

Bake at 375° for 45 minutes.

Cottage Pudding

Contributed by Melissa Nicholson

This was always a favorite dessert in the fall/winter months because it's served warm. My mom would make the chocolate sauce ahead of time and leave it sitting over the hot water in a double boiler. She would pop the cake into the oven just as we sat down to eat dinner (perfect timing to be slightly cool in time for dessert).

1 cup flour
½ cup sugar
⅛ tsp. salt
2 tsp. baking powder
½ cup milk
1 egg
2 tbs. melted shortening

Sift together flour, sugar, salt, and baking powder.
Add milk, beaten egg, and shortening.
Beat well and bake in greased shallow square pan at 400° for 20 minutes (until lightly browned).

Top with chocolate sauce (recipe below). It's also good with a lemon curd sauce.

Chocolate sauce:

3 1-oz. squares unsweetened chocolate
1¾ cups milk or cream
1 cup sugar

¼ cup flour
¼ tsp. salt
1 tbs. butter
1 tsp. vanilla

Melt chocolate in milk (or cream) over pan of hot water (double boiler). Cook until smooth, stirring occasionally.

Combine sugar, flour, and salt. Add enough chocolate mixture to the dry mix and stir into a smooth paste. Add back to the remaining chocolate and blend in.

Cook and stir until smooth and slightly thick (about 10 minutes).

Remove from heat and stir in the butter and vanilla.

Can be left sitting over hot water if you're going to be serving soon. It can also be refrigerated and is delicious on top of ice cream.

Kitty Pretzel

Contributed by Robin Coxon

I think we should have equal time for our feline fur babies. Here's a pretzel just for them.

¾ cup canned tuna fish, drained well
¼ cup warm water
1 tbs. butter, softened
1 cup whole wheat flour

Preheat oven to 300°. In a medium-size bowl, mash canned tuna fish well with a fork. Combine with water and butter. Add flour and mix to form a dough. Divide dough into 24 pieces. Roll each piece into a rope and shape into a pretzel. Place on ungreased baking sheet and bake for 20–25 minutes until lightly browned. Cool 5 minutes, then remove to wire rack until cooled completely. Store in airtight container.

Makes 2 dozen.

Your kitty will say meowvalous.

Kathi Daley lives with her husband, kids, grandkids, and Bernese mountain dogs in beautiful Lake Tahoe. When she isn't writing, she likes to read (preferably at the beach or by the fire), cook (preferably something with chocolate or cheese), and garden (planting and planning, not weeding). She also enjoys spending time on the water when she's not hiking, biking, or snowshoeing the miles of desolate trails surrounding her home.

Kathi uses the mountain setting in which she lives, along with the animals (wild and domestic) that share her home, as inspiration for her cozy mysteries.

Stay up to date with her newsletter, *The Daley Weekly*. There's a link to sign up on both her Facebook page and her website, or you can access the sign-in sheet at: **http://eepurl.com/NRPDf**

Kathi Daley Blog: **http://kathidaleyblog.com**

Facebook at Kathi Daley Books, **www.facebook.com/kathidaleybooks**

Kathi Daley Teen – **www.facebook.com/kathidaleyteen**

Kathi Daley Books Group Page –
https://www.facebook.com/groups/569578823146850/

Kathi Daley Recipe Exchange -
https://www.facebook.com/groups/752806778126428/

Webpage - **www.kathidaley.com**

E-mail - **kathidaley@kathidaley.com**

Recipe Submission E-mail –
kathidaleyrecipes@kathidaley.com

Goodreads:
https://www.goodreads.com/author/show/7278377.Kathi_Daley

Twitter at Kathi Daley@kathidaley -
https://twitter.com/kathidaley

Amazon Author Page –
http://www.amazon.com/author/kathidaley

Pinterest -
http://www.pinterest.com/kathidaley/